# RUNNING
# LOOSE

# RUNNING
## LOOSE
### by
## CHRIS CRUTCHER

GREENWILLOW BOOKS • New York

Library of Congress Cataloging in Publication Data

Crutcher, Chris.
Running loose.
Summary: Louie, a high school senior in
a small Idaho town, learns about sportsmanship,
love, and death as he matures into manhood.
I. Title.
PZ 7.C89Ru 1983      [Fic] 82-20935
ISBN 0-688-02002-X

FOR JEWELL AND CRUTCH

# RUNNING
# LOOSE

# CHAPTER 1

T HE YEAR STARTED OUT pretty smooth. Probably would have ended up that way, too, if Becky had stayed around or if I hadn't quit the football team and made myself look like the Jerk of the Universe, though I still say quitting was the only thing to do, and I wouldn't change that.

I mean, Norm let me buy the pickup at the end of last summer, I had two pretty good jobs so the money was rolling in, and I finally got a starting spot on the football team.

And I had Becky.

I wasn't doing bad in school either. My grades weren't

world-beaters; but two of my senior English compositions were entered in the State Prose and Poetry Fair down in Boise, and the *Daily Statesman* even printed one of them. In fact, some guy from the paper called me long distance to tell me to keep them in mind if I decided to go to college and major in journalism. Got to thinking I was pretty hot stuff. Seemed like all I had to do was shove 'er in neutral and coast on in to graduation. But when it goes, man, it goes.

We play eight-man football in Trout, mostly because in any given year at least two teams in the league couldn't field an eleven-man team without using their cheer-leaders. In Idaho, if your student body doesn't have more than 125 people in it, you can play eight-man ball. Any more than that, you have to play eleven. There's not a school in our league that comes close. This wouldn't be any kind of big deal except that it's real hard for anyone from an eight-man team to get a college scholarship. Most colleges don't even consider it football.

I'm not talking about myself. I couldn't get a football scholarship to Treasure Valley Community College as a blocking dummy the way I play, if you want to be honest about it. But Carter—he's our quarterback and my best friend—and Boomer Cowans—he's our running back and definitely not my best friend—might be good enough. Our team hasn't lost a game in three years, and those guys are the reason. Carter's big and strong and fast and smart, and he can throw the ball a mile. Boomer's bigger and probably stronger and almost as fast and dumber than a cinder block. But he's mean, and you can't hurt him because he doesn't care, and he has a lot of natural instinct for the game. At least that's what Coach Lednecky says. Lednecky's the cinder block that Boomer's dumber than. Me, I'd just try to get a decent catch once in a while and let those guys do their stuff.

Anyway, Carter and Boomer are probably going to get a shot at some college ball next year because we got a lot of press for winning the State Eight-Man Championship three years running and because Lednecky was able to persuade a couple of scouts from C of I and Ricks College to come take a look. He even sent some game films up to the U.

Sometimes I feel kind of sorry for Boomer. I mean, even with all the crap I got into this year, my future doesn't look that bad. I don't think I did anything that can't be fixed, though you might get some argument there from Lednecky or Jasper, who runs this place. I've got a few irons in the fire. But I don't know about Boomer. If he doesn't make it playing ball—which doesn't seem too likely, considering you'd have to add three points to his grade point average to bring it up to an F—he's going to be setting chokers and top-loading his old man's logging truck for the rest of his life or at least until *he* has a kid to do it for *him*. It doesn't seem like there's much of what makes the rest of us shine in Boomer. I mean, the only time he laughs is when someone else is getting screwed. And he's always talking about making it with some girl he's never touched and adding some weirdball garbage that, if it had really happened, would cheapen her. Like he said he took Adrienne Klinner down to the drive-in in Boise, and when she was out going to the bathroom, he poked a hole in the bottom of the popcorn box and stuck Ol' Norton up through. (Boomer's dad doesn't let him cuss—beats him up when he hears it—so Boomer calls his "thing" Ol' Norton.) Anyway, then he held the box in his lap, and when she'd eaten down about halfway (three-quarters would be more like it), she got a handful. Said she shrieked at first, but then she started playing with it and went crazy. Crap like that. He's so dumb he doesn't know every jerk in the world has told that story. I mean, Adrienne Klinner would have poured her Coke into the box and taken a bus back to Trout.

I almost lost my life when I said I didn't believe that story, which is why most of the time I don't feel sorry for Boomer at all, because he scares me to death. I know if I gave him half a reason, he'd tear off my arms and beat me with the bloody stubs. He's hated me ever since we were in grade school and I asked his dad if he really lost his logging truck down a jelly roll. That might sound strange if you don't know what a jelly roll is. None of the streets in Trout is paved, except for Main Street, and every spring we get these frost heaves in them—the road sort of buckles up, and there's this runny mud that comes up just under the surface. Anyway, one of the favorite springtime sports for little kids is to jump up and down on them to soften them up. We were at Boomer's birthday party and were working on one on the road right out in front of his house. Carter said he heard that old Mrs. Grant's oldest kid got swallowed up by one back when our parents were in school. Nobody ever talked about it, and Carter didn't know the guy's name; but he knew it was a true story. Boomer had to go him one better, so he said a jelly roll had sucked up his dad's logging truck two years ago. When I went in to ask his dad if it was really true, he stormed out, grabbed Boomer by the arm, jerked him inside, and proceeded to whip the crap out of him. All we heard was: "I told you, no more stupid lies!" over and over. When Boomer came back out, his face was streaked with tears and his new birthday shirt was torn and he told us we all had to leave. Nobody could believe it. I mean, that's pretty hard core. Annie Creason told us later that his dad threw away all his presents after we left. Anyway, he's hated me ever since. I'm sure if I weren't such good friends with Carter, Boomer'd have laid waste to me years ago.

Getting my part-time job down at the Buckhorn at the beginning of last summer was good. I was already working full time down at Norm's 66 station, and then Dakota offered me a couple of hours a day sweeping the place out and restocking the coolers with beer and replacing empty kegs with full ones. I started at three bucks an hour, and he's given me a couple of small raises. I've worked for Norm for years, so I'm up to four and a quarter there. Norm said when I had enough for a small down payment plus enough to cover insurance, he'd sell me the pickup. I pulled that off in August. Norm's my dad, so gas is free. The pickup is a '52 Chevy that's been treated like one of the family, except for maybe the paint job. Buying it probably wasn't what you'd call a financially astute move, since I could use it anytime I wanted anyway, but we got to be such good friends I thought it ought to belong to me.

It's never betrayed me. Always starts on the first crank no matter what the weather's like. A couple of times last winter, when it got down around forty or fifty below, it was about the only thing in town moving. I'd walk out to the driveway, knowing damn well its thirty-year-old bones were froze up tight, flip the key, hit the starter, and she'd crank right over. 'Course I keep enough antifreeze in it that if Donkey Caulder could figure out how to drain the radiator, he could stay out of the Buckhorn all winter. Donkey's the town drunk.

I guess I'm sort of a wussy, to put it in Boomer's language. A wussy is a cross between a wimp and a word Boomer's dad almost beat him senseless for using. I hate like hell to admit it, but sometimes it sure seems like it must be true. I spend about half my life worrying about hurting other people's feelings and wondering if they like me, though for a while there, there wasn't any wondering to do. I *knew*.

Like one of the reasons I never made it with a girl was I was afraid she'd cry and feel crappy when it was over. I've heard that happens sometimes. And I knew that would make me feel crappy. That's not the kind of information I want spread around, but it's the truth, really. Not that I've had a *lot* of chances—I won't give you a Boomer Cowans and tell you they line up around the block to watch me tuck in my shirt—but there were a few times. With nice girls, too.

And one reason I didn't make it big in football before this year was that I wouldn't cream the little guys in practice. Lednecky always wanted everybody to go all out against everybody, and that meant if you came up against a 95-pounder in the meat grinder, you took his head off. I'm not a big guy—maybe 160—but it doesn't take much against some of those poor suckers he talks into turning out. 'Course when I was a 95-pounder in the ninth grade, nobody let up on me. I guess that's what makes me a wussy. The other reason I didn't make it big in football before this year, like I said, is that I've never been all that good. Not too big, not too fast, and a lot more desire to be a football player than to play football, if you know what I mean. Might as well get that all out in the beginning.

Being a wussy isn't so bad, though, if you can work it into your act. Carter says the most important thing is to get your act down, and he could have a point. He's sure got a good act.

# CHAPTER 2

I<small>N A WAY</small> Becky was probably out of my league. At least in the way a lot of guys would look at it. It was one of those deals where you'd say, "God, she could have any guy she wants. What's she doing with him?" Even I said that. Becky was one of those girls you want so bad it aches— the kind that before you get to know her, you make a real jerk of yourself every time you run into her. You go home and practice what you're going to say and how you're going to act next time, and then you screw it up again.

We probably wouldn't have ended up together anyway. I have this theory about guys and girls and love affairs and

Dakota came in just as we were finishing up. He lives above the tavern in a nice little place he built himself up there, and he always comes down to shoot the breeze about the time I'm through. He's a rugged-looking old fart with a face that looks like a dried-up road and a hook for a left hand. Not one of those hooks that's attached to your nerves and works like a pair of chopsticks; just a hook. Like a pirate. He never finished the fourth grade, but he's real decent and smart as hell.

"Football heroes!" he said. "Coulda used you guys in here last night. Christ. Winnie had to cold-cock ol' Benny Harper to get his grizzly old paws off her, Bill Abbott thought he was ridin' a streak with his carpenter's trick, and things just generally got out of hand. Coulda used ya."

I was making my last swipe over the bar, and Carter was into the beer sausage.

"Better load up on that stuff now," Dakota said. "Soon's you bomb out as a college football hero and flunk outta school, you'll be back here haulin' logs for Caxton, an' those'll cost you a quarter apiece."

Carter reached into the jar and took two more. "When I bomb, I owe you six bits." He spun the lid down tight and snapped his fingers. "Damn," he said. "I forgot my cleats at the gym. I'll run back and get 'em. Meet me over at the field in about a half hour, okay, Louie?"

I nodded and said okay, and Carter trotted out the back door.

Dakota hoisted himself up on the bar while I finished putting the chairs back down. "You guys gonna pull it off again this year?" he asked. He asked me that a lot, al-

that kind of stuff. You want, and maybe need, different things at different times in your life, and you go around looking for somebody that fits. Most times a person that fits in one time of your life won't fit in another time, or like I think it would've been in our case, you won't fit for them. Pretty soon you find yourself with somebody who doesn't do it for you anymore and who needs you like an old fish head. That's probably a good time to wrap it up, but hardly anyone does. I've seen it a lot around town here. People who have been together since high school—or at least since their early twenties. They got nothin' for each other anymore, but they have kids and bills and some crazy idea that the only way to judge a marriage is by how long it lasts. Longevity is what it's called. They're sitting around waiting for each other to croak so the one that's left can call it a success. They're not all like that, but enough to make you not want to run right out and get hitched.

Anyway, like I said, even if Becky had stayed around, we probably wouldn't have gotten married and had kids and a life or anything, but I like to think if it was good while it lasted, it was good. And it was good. Dakota says if we always judged things by how they ended up, life would more than likely seem like one turd sandwich after another, given the way things have a tendency to end up. He's a good man to listen to, if you don't mind a little rough language, which I don't. I'll tell you about Becky sometime.

But first there's football. I told Dakota I'd be a little late to clean up on the Thursday before the first Monday practice. Actually he didn't care what time of morning I came in as long as the place was ready to open by noon, so Carter and I went up to the school to check out our gear first. Seniors get to pick out their stuff a day ahead of everyone else—that is, if they've played all three years before—and Lednecky had talked the school board into a few thousand dollars of new equipment on the basis that we'd been state champs two years in a row. Carter and I were the first ones there and got primo gear.

Then Carter came down to the Buckhorn with me afterward so we could get done quick and go over to the field and run some pass patterns before I had to go to work over at the station. I do the two-till-midnight shift there in the summers.

Carter and I had been working out twice a day all summer so we'd have a jump on everyone from the first day of practice on, for different reasons, though. Before this year, even though I lettered, I never started a game, and I *really* wanted to make it. To hear me tell it now, most times, you'd think it was no big deal. But don't let me fool you. I wanted it bad. Carter always works out like a madman because everybody thinks he's Superman and he doesn't want them thinking any different. Always wants it to look easy. He figures if the team really believes he's a magician, then he is.

The Buckhorn looked a little worse than usual for a weekday. Several glasses were tipped over on the bar, and a couple were broken on the floor behind it. There were chairs turned over and a long crack in the glass on the

front of the jukebox where an empty pitcher had obviou hit it. And there was a pool of dried blood on the bar.

Carter started stacking chairs on tables while I got the broom and mops. "Animals," he said. "These g should be put in cages." He tossed me a glass th caught and set on the bar.

"I've seen it worse," I said. "You oughta come in h sometime on the fifth of July. It looks like the remain the Sheep-eater Massacre. They don't take prisoners.'

He smiled and finished stacking the chairs, then g hand truck to move in new kegs behind the bar. I sw and filled the mop bucket.

"How much do you think that is?" he said, pointin the dried blood on the bar. "You think it's a pint?"

I went over and looked. There were nail holes under blood and to one side. "It's however much blood is in Abbott's right hand," I said. I'd seen it plenty of times fore. Bill had this trick he does sometimes, where he drunk on his butt and takes bets he can drive a sixte penny nail into the bar with his hand. He wraps his around it so the nail is sticking out between the sec and third knuckles and the head rests against the call on the upper part of his palm. When he thinks he ha good grip, he slugs the bar. He's good for about two ou three. I've seen him do it, and when he misses, it's like hand explodes. He sits there cussing while somebody g a car to run him to the hospital for stitches. There's much going on that the other guy usually doesn't ever paid. Donkey Caulder sits there shaking his head and s ing, "Bullshit."

though he really didn't care one way or the other. It was just a way to get the conversation going.

I shrugged. "Hard to say. No one in the league can beat us, but you never know what's going to happen in the postseason." I smiled a little. "To tell you the truth, what I worry about most out there is not screwing up." It's easy to be honest with Dakota; I'm not sure why. "If nobody screws up, Carter and Boomer can take care of most of it. Besides, if I don't screw up, I don't have Lednecky on my butt."

He stared at me and shook his head. "Now what kind of damn attitude is that?" he said. "Not screwing up." He likes me, and it hacks him off when I put Carter and Boomer out of my league or when I put myself down. Says it's just all the farther I have to pull myself back up.

"That attitude is going to make me a starter," I said.

"Big deal. A starter on an eight-man football team from Podunk High School. Hell, just showin' up every day for four years'll get you that." He eased himself down and walked around behind the bar. "You know, Louie," he said, "I kinda got my eye on you. You know that. I don't even care if you play ball at all, but don't go into *anything* just tryin' not to screw up. That's cheap, son. Tell you what. Who do you play first?"

"Tamarack Falls," I said. "Three weeks from tomorrow."

"Okay," he said. "During warm-ups you get over close to their sideline an' pick out the best-lookin' cheerleader they got. Then do somethin' in the game that'll make her remember your number."

I smiled. "I could pick up a fumble and run it into our

own end zone," I said. "Or set a league record for penalties."

"Cute," he said. "I'm here wastin' my valuable time, tryin' to make a man outta you, an' what I get is a smartass. You do what I said. Don't go in there scared of makin' mistakes. You go in there and kick some butt."

I said I'd think on it. Dakota's a funny guy. He runs the down markers at all the games—probably hasn't missed one in twenty years—but he doesn't see it like everyone else. He doesn't care a whole lot about winning or losing—I mean, he's seen a hell of a lot of both in his time—but he cares about how you do if he likes you. I don't know why he picked me out, though he's liked me for a long time, but I do know when Dakota's pulling for you, you don't want to let him down. At least I don't.

I met Carter down at the field around noon, and we jogged a mile to warm up. We usually tossed the ball back and forth while we jogged and shot the bull some. Sometimes we'd do practice drills or run backwards and sideways in short spurts to practice defensive maneuvers. The one I liked best was where Carter would jog along behind me and toss the ball over one of my shoulders or over my head. He'd yell, "Right!" or, "Left!" or, "Top!" to tell me where it was coming from, and I'd see if I could catch it without looking back. He'd yell just before the ball came into my vision. It's a good drill for reflexes, and we did it every day at least once. I was getting pretty good at it. We did it for two laps that day, and I only missed twice.

"Three days till practice starts," he said. "Gotta be ready.

Right!" He tossed the ball over my right shoulder into my outstretched hands. I flipped it back without looking.

"I can see it now," he went on. "Sampson to Banks on a down-and-out—left!—Sampson to Banks on a post. Sampson to Banks on a hook-and-go. Touchdown! Top!"

"Sampson and Banks to Evergreen County Hospital for major surgery," I said, "in the second quarter of the Tamarack game, when Cowans gets tired of Sampson trying to make a hero out of Banks." I flipped it back.

Carter held the ball and caught up to me. "Boomer'll be okay," he said. "You just have to know how to handle him. He ain't smart, but he ain't dumb enough to get me down on him. I mean, who gives him the ball?"

"Got a point," I said. "Me, I know how to handle him. From a distance. Maybe the next county."

Carter did have a point. He always has a point. He knows exactly what he's doing all the time. It's hard for me to figure how he can look so free and easy when I know he calculates every move he makes. I guess it goes along with having a good act.

# CHAPTER 3

I GUESS I GOT a pretty good draw when they handed out parents. I mean, just since last summer Rob Dropzec's uncle became his stepdad while his real dad became his stepuncle in a trade that still has the fans baffled. And Amy Miller's little brother got taken away—*taken away*—because he kept showing up at school with funny bruises and marks on his back and legs. Carter hasn't spent three days with his old man since he was five and his dad took a hotshot job with Morrison-Knudsen down in Boise. He was supposed to move the family down as soon as he got settled in his job and found a house. What he found was a new family, and now it's like Carter doesn't exist. Carter and I ran into him down there one night in a pizza place, and it got pretty heavy; but other than that one time, Carter pretends his dad doesn't exist either. Just says it's no big deal.

And then there's Becky's parents. Her dad is a real class guy, one of those people who seem to know how things work. But his noodle must've been on sabbatical when he married her mom, to hear Becky tell it. Boy, now she's a case for the books. If you could bottle half the garbage she pulls, you could sell it for 150 proof Brain Disease. Luckily they aren't together anymore either. Becky chose to live with her dad when they split a little over three years ago. Her mom stayed back East, where Becky used to live, and her dad came out here to be a frontier lawyer.

And I wouldn't have Boomer's dad if he were the only one left in the world. It's not hard to see where Boomer comes by his sweet attitude. Stuff like what happened that time at his birthday party is just a way of life at his house. And his mom is the only person in the world tough enough to hang in there, though I don't know why she'd want to.

Anyway, except for the times I wish I had crappy parents so I'd have someone to blame things on, I gotta say I got a pretty good deal. Norm's always real calm and takes time to work things out. Doesn't like to leave a lot of loose ends. He's a good guy to go to when you have a problem. He'll never tell you the answer, but he'll stick with you till you come up with one. Brenda's a little more emotional—like to the seventh power—but you need a little of that.

She's good for helping you realize that how you feel is how you feel, and a lot of times there's no use trying to control it. If you lived your whole life like that, you'd probably turn out like Donald Duck, but there's a need for some of it. At least for me there is. And she's full of love. I mean she loves this family like love's the mail. She delivers through rain and sleet and dark of night and conditions that are a whole lot worse than any of those.

Don't get me wrong. We don't live here like the Beaver Cleaver family or the Waltons all the time. Brenda and I go at it pretty regularly. I mean, she's forever doing things like buying me new undershorts to wear when I travel someplace, even if it's just an away game, and throwing away my old ones.

"Louie, I've seen your underpants. I know what you do."

I bet she doesn't know how often.

Just when I get them washed a few times and nice and soft and broken in, they disappear. She says how would I feel if I got in an accident and was wearing some old pair of brown and yellows. Like they're going to identify my body by the stains on my skivvies and leave her to live out her life in total and utter humiliation. I can see the obituary in the *Trout News:*

Died. Louis Frederick Banks (1964–1982). Survived by father (Norman), mother (Brenda), sister (Tracy), and crusty undershorts (Jockey). His mother should be ashamed.

Really, that's the kind of arguments we get into sometimes. I don't know how I get sucked into them, but I do.

Brenda's got heart, though, and you can go through a lot of petty little crap for that.

I don't think I could have gotten through this year alive without my folks. I mean, they didn't actually do anything; but they were always there, and they did surprisingly little judging considering some of the stuff I pulled.

Anyway, I was telling you about football. We started our two-a-day workouts the Monday after we picked up our equipment. It started like every season starts: with us sitting on the bleachers in the gym at seven-thirty in the morning in our jocks and T-shirts waiting for Lednecky to come out of his office up behind the stage to give us the opening pep talk that's supposed to charge us up for the season. Everyone is pretty nervous because those first few practices are hell. We get a "Summer Newsletter" along about the first of July that tells us what kind of condition ("excellent, gentlemen") he expects us to report in, but everybody puts it off till it's too late. We know we're going to have to run the mile right off, and if we don't hit our time—six minutes for backs and ends, eight minutes for linemen—we'll run it at the beginning of practice every day till we do. And if one guy misses, we all run it. ("This is a *team*, gentlemen.") We also know that calisthenics will be triple what they'll be once the season gets going since there's no contact for the first few days until he thinks we're ready and we've all had our physicals. But the killer is the wind sprints. At the end of every practice we run wind sprints until at least four guys throw up. No one believes me. They all think we run a certain number, though only Mark Robeson can say what that number is. ("Infinity, Banks. The predetermined number of wind sprints we run at the end of each practice is infinity. I've counted them.") But I've watched for four years, and when the fourth guy chucks up his breakfast, we head for the showers. In fact, I used to wind them up early by turning away and sticking my finger down my throat right after the third guy went. We'd run one more sprint and go in.

But no more. This year I know I'm ready. Carter and I have been working out all summer—hard. Carter's got me ready to try out for end, Dakota's got me pumped up to make a showing, and I'm ready to run the rest of those would-be athletes into the ground. My target is Boomer. I can't take Carter; he's too fast and in too good a shape. But Boomer's been logging all summer, and though he may be strong and mean enough to eat me if he catches me, I know he can't take me for a mile. No way. So that's my first goal.

Lednecky came down from his office with Coach Madison. This was Madison's first year out of college. He played defensive back at some state college in South Dakota and was pretty hot stuff, I guess. I owe him a lot.

Anyway, Madison sat on the end of one of the bleachers, and Lednecky walked out on the gym floor in front of us. He had his U of I T-shirt and his New York Yankee baseball cap that he swears was given to him by Thurman Munson, who's dead now and can't deny it. As usual, he looked like he could kick any three of our butts with one hand tied to the opposite leg. He's one big strong mother bear.

"Gentlemen," he said, "welcome to Cougar Football. I'll

get right down to it. This is the team I've been waiting for. We've had state champions for the past two seasons, and those were just *building* years. We have six starters back and probably five more who'll be better than the men we lost. We have two boys who will almost certainly receive college scholarships and a couple more who have an outside chance. Man for man, this could be the best team in the state, Triple A teams included." His voice was low and under control, almost like he was talking to somebody on the street, but you could feel the intensity.

"None of us will probably have this opportunity again for a long, long time, if ever." He paused and took off his cap, running his fingers through his H. R. Haldeman haircut. Not even H. R. Haldeman has that haircut anymore.

A lot of guys nodded, but nobody said anything. It wasn't time yet.

It started to build. "We can't allow *anything* to stand in our way this year, gentlemen. We have townspeople who are expecting miracles, we have a school board that put out thirty-five hundred dollars it didn't have for new equipment, and we have pride. For most teams a winning season is considered a success. But for us a nine-and-one season would be a disaster! We're at the very top of the heap! The pinnacle!" he boomed. "Ten-and-O!"

It was time. "Damn right!" Boomer screamed, and everyone joined in chanting, "Ten-and-O! Ten-and-O! . . ."

I suppose if that were on film and we saw it later, we'd all feel like a real bunch of jerks, but luckily the Great Cameraman in the Sky, if there is one, doesn't put you through that. At least I hope not.

Lednecky let it go for a few minutes, then raised his

hand. "All right. Training rules. Same as always. Home by ten, in bed by ten-thirty. Weekends you have until midnight. Night before a game you're home by nine and in bed by nine-thirty. You get one night during the season till two. That's Homecoming. No drinking, no smoking. Tell your girl friends to find something to do for the next two and a half months. You've heard me say it before, and you'll hear it as long as you play for me: You can't do your best in two places. Girl friends will have to wait. Everybody got it?"

"Yes, sir!" we yelled.

"Okay. Break the rules, you're off the team. I don't make exceptions."

I happened to know that was a crock. Carter or Boomer could have shown up at Lednecky's place drunk on their butts at 3:00 A.M. before a game and crawled into bed with his wife and still suited up that afternoon. But those things are understood. For most of us the point was well taken.

Some of the training rules are pretty crazy. Most of them you'd do anyway, whether you were playing football or not, but going to bed at nine-thirty the night before a game is the surest way I know to stay awake all night. And that whole thing about not doing your best in two places never made much sense to me either. Does he think we stop jerking off for two and a half months? I don't. And I do my best, too.

Anyway, Lednecky went on to introduce Madison to us and go over the basic offenses and defenses we would be using. He said he had most of us pegged for the positions he thought we should play, but we were welcome to try out for any we wanted. I said it looked like the only place we were weak was at quarterback, so I thought I'd try out for that. I heard Carter yell, "Top!" but before I could react, a ball hit me in the back of the head. That sort of eased everyone's jitters for a minute.

"Okay," Lednecky said, "if there are no other questions, Coach Madison has your shoes in the equipment room. You can pay as you pick them up. You have twenty minutes to be on the field."

I felt pretty good going onto the field. I was in the best condition of my life, to that point, and I knew no one but Carter was even close. I didn't have to worry about falling in a pile of my own vomit and drowning at the end of the mile. Carter had told me all summer that the reason two-a-days were so rough was that everyone was in such crappy shape, and I believed him. All summer we'd run distances and done wind sprints and push-ups and sit-ups, and I must have run a million pass patterns. I was even starting to develop a little muscle in my chest and arms. No way Lednecky was going to do me in. The only reason I was nervous was I wanted to look good from the first drill to the last; no exceptions. And I wanted to take Boomer in the mile.

I got to the field ahead of everyone and took a couple of easy laps around the track. By the time I'd started my second one Carter fell in beside me.

"Are you ready for this?" he asked.

I nodded. "You bet. What do you figure for this mile?"

"About five-thirty," he said. "No sense killing ourselves

for the rest of practice. Don't worry about time, though. Just go out and kick everyone else's butt, and the time will take care of itself. You want to stay up on everyone."

"What about Boomer?"

"Hasn't worked out all summer, but he's mean enough to be right there with us." He looked over at me and smiled. "It'd kill him if you beat him, though. And it would sure look good to Lednecky."

Mean enough to be with *us*. Carter wasn't going to be with *us*, but he'd decided in early summer he was going to drag me up as far as I'd go. He's a pretty good friend.

The whistle blew, and we headed to the other end of the field to circle the coaches. Sammy Green dropped for fifteen because he took off his helmet and sat on it. ("That damn thing is part of your head for the next three months, Green. Never take it off unless Coach Madison or I tell you to!")

You got the feeling that this was the biggest season of Lednecky's life, including the ones he played. What he'd said in the gym was true. This was the team he'd been waiting for. Probably from the day he crawled out of the La Brea Tar Pits.

We worked through our warm-up calisthenics, and Madison blew his whistle over by the starting line for the mile. Everybody groaned, so we dropped for fifteen. Lednecky said we should look at every challenge as an opportunity for the next three months. He didn't want any crybabies.

"Backs and receivers first," Madison called out. "Get it

under six, guys. It's a lot easier to do it once and get it out of the way." He smiled. "I know you're all in top condition, so it should be a breeze."

Boomer came up behind me and slapped the back of my helmet. "We're a little weak at quarterback, so I think I'll try out for that," he mimicked. "Cute. Christ, I don't see how Sampson can stand you." He slapped my helmet again, interrupting the ringing in my ears from the first time.

"You get this under six, wussy?" he said.

I adjusted my helmet. "I'll be there. Could give you a little push. I'm in pretty good shape."

"That right?" he sneered. "Tell you what, Banks. You take me in this mile, I'll pack your gear for every away game and carry it on and off the bus." He smiled, if you can call what he does smiling. "If I win, you wear my sweaty jock around your nose to Homecoming."

"That's okay, Boomer," I said. "Thanks for the offer, though."

"Screw it," he said. "You beat me, I'll pack your gear."

I knew damn good and well he'd never hold to that if I beat him, but the prospect of watching him worm out of it really jacked me up.

"Whatever you say," I said, and we trotted to the line.

Boomer lined up on the inside with me next to him. The rest of the backs and ends lined up next to us with Carter on the outside. At the sound of the whistle Boomer's foot shot out and tripped me, but I caught myself with my hands and only lost a step or two. Carter came off the line quick and cut to the inside about three or four steps ahead of everyone. I caught up to him. Boomer was a few steps behind.

"Goin' out fast," Carter said. "Stay with me."

I matched him stride for stride, but you could tell it was a lot easier for him than it was for me. We were opening a wide gap between ourselves and the rest of the pack. Only Boomer was hanging close. Carter said the key was to wear everyone down on the first three laps so no one would even try to make a run at the end. The gap widened. Boomer stayed in it.

By the end of the third quarter it looked like we might lap Larry Ingram, and the rest of the guys were strung out around the track. When we crossed the line to start the last lap, Carter said, "You're on your own," and lengthened his stride, picking up speed almost effortlessly. I tried to stay with him for about a hundred yards but there was no way, so I looked around to see where Boomer was. He was hanging in about ten yards back. I couldn't see his face very well inside his helmet, but I thought I caught a quick glimpse of desperation. I picked up a little on the back stretch, knowing that desperate or not, if that scumbag was within fifteen yards of me going into the final turn, he'd just outsprint me. Going into the turn, I thought I heard his footsteps, so I picked up a little more. I could tell it was a good mile because my lungs hurt and my lower gut burned. But time didn't matter; I just wanted to beat that bastard. I picked up a little more. Coming out of the turn, I opened up. I could hear his footsteps coming hard, but I was all out. My gut was on fire, and my legs were like bricks; but I forced it out of my mind. About twenty-five yards from the finish I saw Madison standing with the watch. Carter was finished, and all I could hear was Boomer's feet. I had to hold on! With about ten yards to go, he shot past me like I was standing still, screaming, "Cram it, wussy!"

I finished hard and kept going, easing the pace to a trot. Carter fell in beside me. "Good run," he said. "Under five twenty. He got you on the kick."

I looked back to see Boomer bent over the ditch outside of the track with his helmet in his hand, heaving his guts out. I thought about asking Lednecky why he didn't have to drop for fifteen for taking off his helmet, but not for long. I was gasping for air, but I wasn't sick.

"Jesus," I said between gasps, "you don't beat him easy. I had it turned on all the way. He must really hate me."

"That would explain it," Carter said. "Maybe you're lucky you didn't take him. It might not have been worth it."

The whistle blew, and we turned around and jogged back. The linemen were running their mile, and Lednecky took us over to run some pass patterns. Larry Ingram and Allen Snyder were the only ones who didn't make the six minutes, but that meant we'd have to run it every day until they did or until Lednecky gave it up. Christ, Larry Ingram couldn't do a six-minute mile in a car.

I'd have plenty of chances to take Boomer in the mile, and I did every time after that because he just ran with the pack. He'd shown his stuff, and it wasn't worth the pain now that I knew.

The rest of the practice went well. I found out that what had seemed like calculated torture for the past three years was only a good workout if you were in shape, just like Carter said. The wind sprints were tough, and four guys chucked up before we were through; but I was up front on all of them and even took Carter on a couple where he was getting his wind. Boomer ate me up on the first five just to let me know how it was and then dropped back with the pack for the rest.

I felt good heading back to the lockers, all things considered. Losing to Boomer hacked me off some, but then there was never any question about which of us had the talent. Measured up against myself and the rest of the mortals, though, I looked pretty good.

# CHAPTER 4

WHEN SCHOOL STARTED and two-a-days were just a miserable memory, we started looking forward to playing some actual football. By that time I'd nailed down the end position and also a linebacker spot on defense. Goin' both ways. Lednecky and Madison were really impressed by my attitude, and I was silently thanking Dakota for building a fire under me. My status with Lednecky seemed to be a rung or so below Boomer and Carter, so I was feeling pretty cocky, like one of the guys that makes things happen. I did my share of dumb-butt things related to that—

forgetting what size pond I was in a lot of the time—but all in all, I handled it pretty well. I mean, I never came right out and bragged all over the place like some guys, though I think I did develop a little Clint Eastwood hitch in my walk there for a while.

And I had it bad for Becky. Who didn't? Every guy in school was in love with her. You were considered weird or homo or something if you weren't. But I had it bad. Worse than bad. I talked to her a few times—every chance I got—and I saw her out on the field, practicing with the other cheerleaders, and she was pleasant enough; but I couldn't tell if she liked me or anything. Carter usually helped me out on the field by giving me at least one diving attempt at a ball he'd fire within inches of where they were practicing, but it was just hard to get anything going.

God, she was something. Tall—about five feet nine inches—and strong with long dark brown hair and these green eyes that made you ache. Smarter than hell, and she could get you to do anything she wanted with a smile. You would've thought she'd have ended up with Carter. He's about the only guy that would dare consider himself in her league, except for Boomer, and *he'd* consider himself equal to anyone he could conjure up a wet dream over, which I would say includes every girl in town and several barnyard animals. He sort of works on a sliding scale.

Anyway, I didn't have a lot of close contact with her until Thursday of that first full school week, when she walked right up to me over by the book lockers and asked if I'd like to have a Coke with her after the Tamarack Falls game, which was the next day. She walked right up and asked me that. It didn't embarrass her or anything, at least not that I could see. To tell the truth, I'd have walked across ten thousand miles of burning sand in my bare feet to see her cheerleader panties go by in a laundry truck, as Dakota says, but I was pretty cool, all things considered, and said yeah, I'd like that.

The Tamarack Falls game was a romp. Boomer ran for two touchdowns in the first quarter, and by half time we were up 35–zip. I didn't score any points, but I had three receptions, one that was nothing but class when I caught a perfect strike at the three-yard line just as two of their guys high-lowed me. Carter said I landed on my head. I held onto the ball, though, and Boomer went over on the next play. None of the first-stringers played much of the second half, and I found myself thinking way more about having a Coke with Becky than football by the time the fourth quarter started.

In the locker room everyone was pretty high. People were laughing and joking about the great plays they'd made, and Lednecky came in and gave us an extra hour that night. There was supposed to be a record dance in the gym, and he was letting us stay till the end.

Boomer made sure all the second-stringers were branded on the butt with a welt from his towel before they got out, in case they should get the idea that they were anywhere near his league. He included me in on that; by mistake, he said.

Becky was waiting by the gym door when I came out. She walked up and said, "Nice game," and slipped her arm inside mine. Right there in front of everybody. Made me feel like a star. Boomer saw it, and I knew that later I'd have to hear about the infinite number of times he'd screwed her; but even that couldn't begin to spoil the moment.

Carter went by and slapped me on the butt and said, "See you tomorrow," and was gone. Usually I gave him a ride home, and I would have that day, too, if he'd wanted one; but he just wanted out of my way. Up until this last year I was pretty slow with the ladies, and that's not the half of it, and he knew that. Hell, in a town of nine hundred people everyone knew it, but Carter was always real sensitive to it and never gave me a bad time unless we were alone. I appreciated that. But I still wouldn't have minded giving him a ride home.

So Becky said right off, "Listen, why don't you call your mom and tell her you won't be home for dinner? We'll have a burger down at the Chief and then go up to the dance later. My treat."

"I've got money," I said.

"So what? This is my date. I ask you out, I pay. Then you feel guilty and ask me out. Then you can pay. That's how budding romance blooms. Don't worry, it'll all work out."

I shrugged. "Okay, but do me a favor and don't ever tell Boomer you paid."

She smiled. "I wouldn't tell Boomer if his house were on fire."

I started to open the passenger door to the pickup, but she beat me to it.

"Hungry?" she asked.

It was only about five. "Not yet. Wanna go for a ride?" She did.

I stopped at the only phone booth in town to call Brenda and say I wouldn't make it for dinner.

"But I already have your meat out of the freezer," she said.

"Well, can't you put it back in?"

"You can't refreeze meat after it's been thawed," she said.

"I read in the paper where you can," I said. "Go ahead and put it back."

"So what's so important you have to miss dinner?" she asked.

I hadn't been ready to tell her, but I guess I knew she'd ask. "I sort of have a date," I said.

"A date? With a girl?"

"Yes, Brenda, with a girl." I laughed. "Your one and only son and fifty-fifty bet to bring you healthy grandchildren and carry on the noble name of Banks is all right after all. Gave us quite a scare there, didn't he?"

"Never a doubt in my mind," she said. "Who's the lucky lady?"

"Becky Sanders."

"Becky Sanders?"

"Is there an echo in here? Yeah, Becky Sanders."

"Well," she said, "you run along and have a good time.

If I can't refreeze the meat, I'll cut it up for stew tomorrow."

"Brenda," I said.

"What?"

"I have on new undershorts."

She hung up.

We drove out of town about a mile to the reservoir. It was low, and the spillway at the dam was only open about a quarter, so only a little more than a trickle swept into the river below. It was still pretty warm out, and the trees were just beginning to turn. I tried to think of something semiromantic to say about that but caught myself. I'd long since used up my quota of dumb-butt things to say to Becky. I'd do one pretty much every time I ran into her.

We stopped at the spillway for a while and dropped rocks and leaves and spit down into the water. I told Becky how Carter and I used to come up here during fishing season after we'd caught our limit, when the spillway was open full blast, and drop cardboard boxes of fish guts into the torrent below. When they reached the bottom of the spillway, they'd shoot up into the air like a ski jumper out of control and fly all over, showering the fishermen down there on the rocks with the entrails of the very prize they sought. Then we'd haul ass. Becky thought that was pretty funny once I'd assured her that both Carter and I had since put away such childish notions. She also said if I ever wanted to try it again, for old times' sake, to give her a call. Then she put her arms around my neck and gave me a big hug. I didn't get it; but I sort of hugged her back, and I gotta say it felt pretty good.

We drove around the lake a ways farther, up past the old Crown Point cemetery and the rock crusher onto some old logging roads that wind back up into the hills like they're going someplace. Nobody's logged back there for years, so the only people who use them are hunters and kids looking for a place to make out. Man, you can lose yourself back there.

Becky had moved over close, and her hand was on my leg. We talked about the game and about loggers and hunters and how many really young people were buried in the old cemetery. Life must have been hard back then. And we talked about the animals that lived there and how they sometimes could tell whether you just wanted to look at them or blow their butts to smithereens. Becky gave them a lot more credit than I did. She said she thought a lot of animals could tell by the way you are. I said from the number of deer and elk and bear you see coming out of those hills draped over somebody's car, a lot of them were exercising pretty bad judgment.

Becky said maybe so.

We stopped at the end of one of the few roads that doesn't circle back to the main road but stops in a wide meadow. It hadn't been used in so long that the turn-around area was grown over. We got out and walked to a big yellow pine that stands right about in the middle. I still don't know why nobody ever logged it. I mean, you could build a whole damn house out of it.

The sun was barely above the hill, and it was cooling down pretty quick. We sat down at the base of the tree, and Becky scootched in close and put her hand in mine. My stomach danced a little, and my heart was negotiating for space with my Adam's apple; but I decided when the shadow of the tree reached the stump in front of the pickup, I'd put my arm around her. The shadow got there. Becky picked up my arm and slipped under. I was *so* smooth.

"I gotta ask," I said finally, breaking the silence.

"What?"

"Why me?"

"Why you what?"

"Who's on first?" I said, but she didn't get it. "Why do you want to spend time with me? I mean, you must know you could have any guy in school. With guys like Carter and Johnny Campbell and Mark Johnson around, why me?"

"You complaining?"

"Unh-unh, sister. No, siree. Not me. Just curious."

"Because if I were an animal in these woods and I saw you here, I'd come up to you."

I didn't have an answer for that.

"How about you?" she asked after a while.

"How about me what?"

"Well, do you like me?"

"Is a five-pound robin fat? Is a bullfrog watertight? Do da Pope wear a beanie?" I caught myself. "You're not Catholic, are you?"

She smiled. "Even if I were, the Pope wears a beanie."

"Okay," I said.

She nodded. "Good. I don't want to be wasting my time."

The sun dropped completely behind West Mountain, and the air cooled off even more, so we headed back to the Chief for burgers. She paid.

# CHAPTER 5

M ONDAY before the Salmon River game I was on top of the world. Friday night with Becky had been like some kind of dream or something. I couldn't have wished for a better setup. We went to the Chief and ate, then up to the dance for a while. I didn't have to hold up the walls. I was *with* somebody. And we danced every slow dance together (Norm calls them belly dances). When someone would come up and ask her to dance, she'd say I had already asked and lead me out on the floor. The chaperons are supposed to walk around during the slow ones and make sure there's light between each couple, but Becky had that system beat. She'd dance me off into the dark corner and, whenever she saw one of them coming, would dance back a step and push me gently away. When they left, she'd come in real close again and put her head on my shoulder. I was going nuts! And we never got caught once. That method is Jasper's way of making sure we don't conceive on the dance floor, but most of the chaperons don't pay too close attention to it. Jasper's our principal and superintendent, and he's from the hard-ass school of principals and superintendents.

We left early—Becky told everyone that a good athlete needs his rest—and drove the pickup back out to the meadow. The moon was past three-quarters, so you could see the grass and the long shadow of the tree. We hugged and kissed and held each other for a while—she kept it all under control—and then I took her home. Made it a half hour before team curfew.

Saturday she came down to the station and washed her dad's car and kept me company. I asked her if she wanted my letter sweater, but she said she didn't think that was necessary. I was kind of relieved. You pay fifty dollars for the thing; then you don't get to wear it because you give it to your girl friend, who it looks like hell on, unless she's a monster, in which case she probably looks like hell anyway. Becky said it all smacked of ownership, and that wasn't the kind of relationship she had in mind. I was pretty much along for the ride, so it didn't matter to me.

What a ride.

I guess if you had to pick a day where things started

falling apart, you'd have to go with that Monday.

Mr. McElroy, the shop teacher, is an amateur photographer, so we have some makeshift game films, like the big time. He ain't great—sometimes he'll zero in on the ball and then, after it's snapped, you stare at the spot in the grass where it was hiked from while the play goes on un-noticed—but they're certainly better than nothing. Once last year he caught me missing a tackle and then just left the camera on me while I laid in the grass with my chin in my hands and the turkey I missed went on to score. That was the day I learned Lednecky's definition of "pursuit."

Anyway, after the films Lednecky called us to the bleachers in the gym, which was unusual. When we were all sitting and quiet, he took off his hat and sailed it over by the stage and said, "Gentlemen, we had a fine game Friday. There weren't many mistakes, and none that were costly. And Coach Madison and I got a good chance to look at some of you younger men. So let's just look ahead."

He ran his hand over his face like he does when he's real serious. "Salmon River beat Connelly sixty-three to six. Now Connelly doesn't have much, and we probably could have run up the same kind of score against Tamarack Falls if we'd poured it on. But Salmon River has a transfer from down in California somewhere that we'll have to watch out for. He's a black kid, a Negro. Name's Washington, and he scored six touchdowns."

There were a few low whistles, and guys glanced around at each other.

"That's right," he said. "Six TDs." He paused. "And he's

their quarterback. He passed for two more." His voice dropped a little. "Men, I don't know exactly where this boy came from, but we can't afford to let a ringer come in and spoil everything we've worked for. Now I don't want to sound prejudiced; but I played with blacks up at the U, and there's only one way you can stop them. That's to hurt 'em. And I'm telling you now, and I don't want it to leave this room, I want that Washington kid out of the game! Early!" His voice was no longer low, and the veins in his neck and forehead looked like a road map. His face looked like he was having a heart attack. The man was serious.

"Kill that jungle bunny!" Boomer screamed.

"Yeah! Yeah!" Guys were going nuts.

Lednecky just turned around and took a couple of steps away. I looked over at Carter, who looked back and shrugged. Coach Madison was sitting at the end of the lower bleacher, staring at his shoes. I thought he looked embarrassed.

I couldn't believe it! Lednecky was telling us to go out there and deliberately play dirty football, and everyone was eating it up. To tell you the truth, I was real confused.

Lednecky stepped forward again, raising his hands for quiet. "Okay," he said. "Now besides that, we're still going to have to go out and play good football, so let's hit the field."

I was one of the first ones out, jogging around the track to warm up. Carter fell in with me about halfway through the first lap. Lednecky had given up making us run the mile every day to get Larry Ingram's time under six minutes—

he'd never made it under seven and a half—but I always liked to get a little distance in by myself. It loosened me up, and I usually used the time to get psyched up for practice. That day I was just using it to figure.

"What do you think?" I asked Carter.

"About what?"

"About Lednecky giving us thumbs-down on that black kid. Sounds kinda low to me. I mean, we've got a good team; we shouldn't have to pull that kind of crap."

"Aw," Carter said, "forget it. Coach gets a little wound up sometimes. He doesn't really mean anything by it."

"Tell Boomer that."

Carter laughed and shook his head. "Yeah, that's for sure. What the hell, though, if the guy's as good as Lednecky says, we won't be able to catch him to hurt him."

The whistle blew, and we headed in.

I was hoping Coach would let it drop, but he harped on Washington the rest of the day. The defense was set up to key on his every move. He was by far their best athlete, and he played quarterback, so that wasn't unusual; but still, a lot of talk was about how to put him out of commission. Boomer was thriving on it. It seemed to give his life new meaning. I got into an argument with him about it after practice—I can be such a dumb-butt at times—and almost cut my life short. He was talking about "sending all them grrs back to Africa on a leaky boat," and for some reason I felt the urge to lay out what I'd learned about civil rights— in Lednecky's government class, for Christ's sake—for him.

"You ever had any problem with blacks, Boomer?" I asked.

50

"Damn right," he said. "Bunch of 'em jumped my old man once. In a service station can. There was four of 'em. Had knives, too."

"What'd they do?"

"Took every damn thing he had, buttbreath. What the hell's it to ya? You some kinda nigger lover?"

"Geez," I said, "I don't know. Only one I ever met was an editor down at the *Statesman*. He seemed nice enough."

Boomer started toward me. The boy's got *no* sense of humor. I was looking for Carter, whose job it is to keep me alive in tough situations. "You don't know what you're talkin' about, Banks. An' I get sick of your smart mouth."

"Come on, Boomer," I said, putting my hands up for protection. "I'm just saying it seems like a raw deal to give a guy just because he's black."

He stopped and threw his towel in my face. "If I was Coach, I'd get rid of you, wussy. If you're too yella to help out the team, why don't you get out? Go hop in the sack with Sanders. I did."

"Hey, screw you, Boomer," I said. The mention of Becky's name made me forget who I was and how dearly I loved life.

"Oh, yeah?" he said, and his right hand came across my face with a loud pop. My four front teeth, which are on a bridge, flew across the room. I lost them to a baseball bat when I was a freshman.

Carter stepped out of the shower. "Hey, what the hell's going on?" he yelled.

I was standing away from Boomer with blood trickling out of my nose and a big gap in the front of my face. My cheek burned, and I hated that scumbag's guts.

"Wussy here thinks he's a damn silver rights leader," Boomer said.

I didn't bother to correct him.

Carter looked over at me. "Jesus Christ, Boomer, just play the game. We're not a lynch mob."

Boomer stood and stared at him for a second. "You heard what Coach said. Maybe you're a nigger lover, too."

Carter stood his ground. "Maybe I am."

For the past year or so Boomer hasn't been sure he could take Carter, and he wasn't about to try unless he knew. Carter understood what that was about and used it all the way. And even if Boomer could take him, he'd get hurt doing it.

"Well, screw you too, Sampson," Boomer said finally, and picked up his towel.

Carter went over to the corner and picked up my teeth, which were miraculously in one piece. "Keep these in your mouth," he said, handing them over. "You're ugly without them."

When I got home for dinner, I was cooled down, but I still couldn't get the whole deal with Washington off my mind. Lednecky had come into the lockers just after Boomer and I got into it to remind us that what he'd said was not to leave that room, and that included our parents; but I didn't pay any attention to that because when I have a problem, I take it home or I take it to Dakota. I mean, I'm not a goody-goody or anything, but the whole thing was ruining my idea of what sports were supposed to be about.

I got out of the pickup to see my sister, Tracy, sitting on the porch steps.

"Your night to do the dishes," she said. Tracy's nine. Usually that means she's good for a bribe. I went for sympathy first.

"Come on, Trace. I'm a football hero. Football heroes don't do dishes. They get battered and sore, and they need their rest. Usually their sisters do the dishes for them."

"Fat chance," she said. "I'll bet Carter does the dishes."

"You know," I said, "we were just talking about that today, as it happens. He says he never does the dishes. Messes up his hands for handling the ball."

"Let's call and ask," she said. She's always had a crush on Carter and would do anything to get to talk to him.

"Okay," I said. "Carter does dishes. How much?"

"Fifty cents."

I fished out two quarters and flipped them to her. She caught them and stuck them in her pocket. "Should have held out," she said. "I would have done it for twenty-five." She went inside.

Norm was already eating, and Brenda was putting mine on. I pecked her on the cheek as I went through to wash my hands. Norm looked up from the paper and nodded.

"So how's it going?" he said when I sat down at the table.

"Okay, I guess." Then I told about Lednecky's plan and my run-in with Boomer.

Norm smiled and shook his head. "Boomer," he said. "I

hope that boy makes it in football. Vietnam ended too soon for him to be a productive citizen there." He put the paper aside. "I wouldn't worry about Lednecky. He gets pretty excited sometimes. I think this will blow over before Friday."

"That's what Carter says," I said, "but I don't know. You should have heard him. It's like it's part of the game plan. I'm really having a hard time with it. I mean, maybe I should quit."

Norm looked up and frowned. "You serious?"

"I don't know."

"Well," he said, "do what you have to, but I wouldn't overreact if I were you. You've worked pretty hard for this season. I'd let it sit for a couple of days."

That's the way Norm is. He's always counseling me to look things over before I do some knee-jerk thing I'll be sorry for. There's nothing wrong with making a mistake as long as you think about it first, but it's stupid to make mistakes by closing your eyes and gritting your teeth. Makes sense.

I did let it sit, and nothing more was said through the week, at least not by Lednecky. We had a lot of hard contact on Tuesday and Wednesday and worked like crazy on our defense. Thursday, as usual, we went without pads and ran plays against dummies. Boomer brought Washington up a few times, usually right after he'd torn some second-stringer's head off by blocking the dummy too high; but Lednecky didn't say a word, and I thought it really had blown over, like Norm said. And I was getting up, no question about it. Salmon River was the only team standing in the way of our making it to the championship game again.

Friday dawned cool and clear. I love Trout on a good game day in the fall. The smoke from the stack down at the sawmill runs straight up in a long white cloud. The trees are turning yellow and red, and the temperature, usually in the low forties or high thirties early, will get up to sixty or so by game time. Carter and I get up early and drive up to the spillway and around the lake, and talk about the game and sometimes our lives.

The whole town shows up for the game. I mean, after two o'clock you can't even buy a beer, or a tank of gas. People close everything up. The few who don't stand out on the sidewalk and listen for cheers. This is a real football town.

School lets out at one-thirty so all the kids can be there in plenty of time for the two o'clock kickoff. The pep club decorates my pickup with purple and gold crepe paper and sells popcorn and peanuts and candy bars and cold pop packed in a big icy galvanized tub, out of the back.

The cheerleaders get out early to get the crowd worked up. I've seen sixty-year-old ladies join in the yells. There's only one small set of bleachers, for the pep band and old people. Everyone else follows the game up and down the sideline, so people come early to get a good place to stand. By the time we blast out onto the field from between the goalposts, you'd think we were the Roman army returning from a three-year stint conquering the known world. It would be hard not to get psyched when you hear that crowd.

We were going through our preliminary calisthenics when the Salmon River bus pulled up. They had suited up at home, I guess to avoid any contact with us before the game. I watched closely as each guy got off, straining to see which one was their secret weapon. No strain was necessary, number 18 was our man. Boy, was he smooth. I suppose I got the feeling a lot of guys get when they see Carter step off the opposing team bus. There's something about the way a special athlete moves that leaves no doubt. Washington seemed to float when he ran. And he threw the ball like Carter, like there was no effort involved, like he'd been born practicing the motion.

Boomer was practicing his kicking over near the sideline with his back to Salmon River. He wouldn't look at them. I looked over at Carter and saw him standing with his helmet off, just watching Washington. And he was smiling.

# CHAPTER 6

SALMON RIVER WON the toss and elected to receive. In the team huddle before the kickoff, Lednecky went down on one knee. "This is it, men. The only thing standing between us and a state championship game at the end of the season is number eighteen. Without him, we could walk away from these guys by three touchdowns. Now here it is. Play him tough. Key on him. Bottle him up on every play. Every time he hits the line, ball or not, tackle him." He paused. "And if you get a clear shot, you better damn well take it."

He put his hand out into the middle of the huddle. The hands of every team member joined it. "Okay," he said. "Let's go win a football game."

A roar went up from the huddle as we broke and the kickoff team took its place on the field.

Lednecky was right about number 18 hurting us. What he did on the kickoff was run it back for a touchdown. In my four years at Trout nobody's ever done that to us. He took the ball around the six-yard line and started straight upfield. My job on kickoffs is to come down wide on the left side and make sure the ballcarrier doesn't get outside me. Boomer, who kicks the ball, comes straight down the middle and destroys anyone who might be stupid enough to come that way. Washington came within three yards of him and cut to my side. I thought I had him contained, especially when he started to my outside and I could use the sideline. I lowered my head to tackle him out of bounds and got air. He just opened up and blew by me. Carter had to come clear across the field and couldn't get there. Washington went in untouched.

Lednecky went nuts. On the sideline he was banging on my helmet, screaming, "You gotta contain! You gotta contain!"

Boomer just glared at me.

Carter slapped me on the butt. "Forget it," he said. "We'll just kick away from him next time."

"He won't be there next time," Boomer said, and pulled his helmet back on.

Carter caught Boomer about halfway back to the field and stopped him. "Listen, Boomer," he said, "let's forget about the sniper tactics and play these guys heads-up."

"You goin' belly-up on us, Sampson?" Boomer said.

"No, but if we play him to hurt him, that means we think he's better than us. And I don't think he's better than us."

He slapped Boomer on the side of the helmet and trotted to his position.

Carter took the kickoff and got us pretty good field position. He started with some short passes to the flats—I caught two—and then pitched out to Boomer on their forty for a thirty-yard gain. He went in on an option to tie the score. We traded two more touchdowns before the half, but we failed to convert on one, so we went in down 21–20.

On nice days we take halftime in the end zone rather than going back to the lockers, so we were lying on the grass, propped up on our helmets, while Lednecky and Madison went around telling different people what adjustments to make. Then Lednecky signaled for silence.

"Men," he said, "overall we're playing some good ball. Other than Banks missing Washington on that first kickoff, there have been no glaring errors, and you've made up for that, Banks. Now we can go on trading touchdowns with these guys, and whoever scores last will win it. *Or* we can do that damn Washington kid in and blow them out! Men, we *have* to win this game."

I figure someday some writer from *Life* magazine or *Reader's Digest* is going to come around and look up Boomer's old teachers and classmates, like they did with

Charles Manson and any number of hillside stranglers or turnpike snipers, and ask us if we ever in our wildest dreams imagined that Boomer would turn out to be a mass murderer. I'm going to say yes, in my daily dreams. I'm going to say that the only thing that surprises me is that he didn't do it sooner. And with his bare hands. Then I'm going to leave the country.

"He won't make it through the third quarter," Boomer said, in a tone that was just plain scary.

I looked over at Carter, who was staring off downfield, where Salmon River was warming up for the second half. He wanted to win this clean, so he was getting his mind off this garbage conversation. By now he was pretty sure that no matter how much Boomer and Lednecky carried on, there was no way they could realize their ambition because no one was going to get a clean shot at Washington anyway. He was too damn quick. It was, to date, Carter's biggest challenge, and he was up for it. I noticed Coach Madison was out of it, too, off to the perimeter, reinforcing taped ankles and talking to guys about their assignments.

We huddled quickly, broke, then went out to warm up.

Carter received the kickoff but couldn't get anywhere with it—or get anything going on the first set of downs—and Boomer had to punt. A lot of guys think Boomer got his name from the way he hits the line after a hand-off, but actually that's not true. He got it for the way he punts. On a good day he could kick the ball to Seattle.

He blasted a high, soaring spiral all the way from our thirty to their fifteen. It bounced out of bounds on their nine. Then Washington went to work. He completed a couple of short passes and ran options to midfield. On a third-and-about-five he rolled out to the right—to the short side of the field—looking for the long pass. Boomer blitzed through the other side and zeroed in on him. Washington stretched it out all the way to the sideline in front of their bench and finally unloaded a bomb. Just as he released, Boomer planted his head in his sternum, lifted him up, and slammed him into the bench. Salmon River players scattered when they saw it coming, and the empty bench caught him just above the kidneys. I heard a low moan and the air leaving his lungs.

Boomer stood up and turned around. "That oughta do it," he said, and walked back onto the field.

That was the last play of my football career. I threw my helmet off and looked at the ref. No call.

"Did you see that?" I screamed.

The ref was Arney Todd from the hardware store. "Did I see what? What are you talking about?"

The other ref, a guy I didn't know from Modoc, was bending over Washington along with Salmon River's coach. Out on the field our players were congratulating Boomer, except for Carter, who came over to see Washington.

I grabbed the other ref. "Did you see that?" I screamed again. "He did that on purpose! He tried to kill him!"

Arney was hollering for Lednecky, who came on the run.

"Better get control of your boy, Coach," Arney said.

Lednecky grabbed me by the collar of my pads. "Banks, what the hell are you doing?"

"He tried to kill him!" I screamed. "And you set it up!" I turned back to Arney. "It was part of the game plan!" I yelled.

"Don't be ridiculous," Lednecky said quietly. "That was a good clean hit. Unfortunate, but clean. How is the boy, Arney?"

"Bullshit!" I yelled. "Really, Arney, it was a setup! It was a stupid, ugly, scummy setup!"

"You need to control his language, Coach. I'll have to call something."

Lednecky pulled me away. "Banks," he whispered, "you shut your mouth, or you'll never play another down of Trout football."

I got loose long enough to pick up my helmet. "Are you kidding me?" I yelled. "I wouldn't play another down of Trout football if you were holding my mother hostage! That was a setup, and you know it!"

Lednecky clamped down on my shoulder pads again. "Banks, you don't have the stomach for this game. Hit the showers."

I looked up, and Boomer was standing there. "Keep it up, wussy," he said.

Carter was behind me. "Take it in, Louie. We'll work it out later."

I stared at him, and he nodded toward the gym. "Go on, take it in."

"You said not to take it seriously. You said—"

"Come on, Louie, take it in." He put his hand on my back and guided me toward the gym. "We'll work it out later."

Boomer started to say something else, but Carter said, "Shut up, Cowans. If you ever want to see the ball again, just shut up," and Boomer shut up.

Lednecky didn't say anything either, I think because he sensed Carter was on the edge. And Carter was running things.

I headed back toward the gym. When I passed the defensive huddle, someone said, "Screw you, Banks," but I couldn't tell who.

When I got to the sideline, I looked back across the field, and Washington was on a stretcher being put into the back of Doc Hamilton's Ford station wagon. I threw my helmet as far back onto the field as I could and headed in.

In the locker room I showered in about three minutes, left my pads and uniform on the floor, and split. In a move that I'm sure got me nominated for Mr. Congeniality of Evergreen County, 1981–82, I went back out to the field, tore all the crepe paper off my pickup, kicked the pep club girls out of the back with their popcorn and peanuts, and turned the tub full of pop over on the ground, breaking most of the bottles.

Becky stepped up on the running board and put her

hand on my wrist and said, "Do you need me?"

I stopped and put my head down. "I don't know what I need," I said. "Better leave me alone for a while. I'll call you tonight."

"Okay."

I roared off.

# CHAPTER 7

TROUT WON THE GAME. I guess we scored a couple of quick ones after they carried Washington off and Salmon River lost their punch. At least that's what Norm and Dakota said. I didn't catch it firsthand.

The Buckhorn was closed for the game, but I have a key, so I let myself in the back way. Donkey Caulder was sitting propped up against the back of the building, drinking something out of a paper bag, shaking his head, and saying, "Bullshit." I couldn't have agreed more.

I got a couple of quarters out of the till, used one to punch up a little Emmy Lou on the jukebox and the other to rack up the balls on the pool table. The shades were pulled, and it was pretty dark, so I turned on the light over the table and hit the switch that activates the beer signs, lighting up the Land of Sky Blue Waters and setting artesian water pouring over the falls. Dakota has these inserts you can put into the pockets to stop the balls from dropping all the way down, so he can shoot pool with his friends for free. Most times I don't need them, to tell you the truth, because I can't get the damn balls in the pockets anyway, but I put them in. Dakota says the best value for your dollar in these days of inflation and exaggerated prices is to play pool with Louie Banks. Takes forever. I guess I have missed a few easy shots in my time. Anyway, while Emmy Lou was having "sweet dreams" about me, I hacked around the table. I thought about pouring myself a shot of Jack Daniel's that Dakota keeps under the bar for private use but decided that might be taking it a little far.

It's funny what goes through your head when major things happen in your life, or at least things that you think are major. Like I was thinking how hard it would be to go buy something at Arney's hardware store and how I'd avoid that if I could. And wondering if one of the second-stringers would get my uniform. I decided they'd probably retire it. I was thinking about regular things, too, like whether I'd made such a jerk out of myself that the whole town would stop talking to me. And how it would affect Norm and Brenda. And what Dakota would say. And whether Boomer Cowans would look me up. One thing I was sure about was Becky. The other thing I was sure about was that Lednecky was a turdhead, and nothing could make me go back or say I was sorry. It was too bad Trout was so small and there wasn't another school I could go to so I'd never have to lay eyes on that scumbag again.

I wondered how Carter could rationalize staying on the team and what Coach Madison was thinking. He never seemed to go for any cheap crap, though he was pretty quiet about it.

I didn't want to talk to anybody, so when I heard the band off in the distance strike up "Under the Double Eagle," like they do after every win, I locked her up and headed up across the spillway, past Crown Point and out to the meadow where Becky and I had gone. I had a conversation with the tree, where I told it how things were going to be from now on, by God, then hiked up the side of the hill and sat on an old dead log and felt sorry for myself.

I got home late for dinner. Trace met me at the door and said she'd do the dishes for free. I told her that wouldn't be necessary, that I wasn't a football hero anymore, but she said she wanted to anyway. That was the first sign that there'd been a powwow. They were going to let me talk about it when I was ready.

I went and washed my hands and sat down at the table while Brenda put my dinner on. Norm was finished and was sitting there with the paper, but I could tell he wasn't reading it.

"Becky called," Brenda said. "She asked to have you call tonight."

I nodded. "Okay," I said, "I'll call her right after dinner."

Norm put down the paper.

I shrugged. "I couldn't help it," I said. "It was a setup all the way. I couldn't believe Arney didn't make a call."

"Maybe he didn't see it that way," Norm said. "It doesn't seem to me like Arney's the problem here."

"Yeah," I said, "but they probably shouldn't let you ref in your hometown."

"Probably not." He passed me some meat. "So, what are you going to do now?"

"I'm going to school, tell anybody who asks me that I think Lednecky's a hunk of slime, break every training rule he ever thought of, and stay the hell away from Boomer Cowans."

Norm smiled. "Sounds like you have a full life planned."

"From now on, I'm a lover," I said.

He nodded and said that didn't sound like a bad alternative and pulled out his pipe. He loaded it with this special cherry-smelling tobacco he only uses after dinner and set the pipe down by his plate. He never smokes while somebody is eating.

"Do what you have to do," he said after a while. "You know your mom and I are behind you, even when we don't agree with you. In this particular case, I do, if that means anything."

It did.

I finished eating and called Becky. She asked how I was doing and if I wanted to drive over to Clear Lake and go bowling or see the movie or something. I sure as hell did.

Before I left, Carter called, just to check in, I guess, and make sure I hadn't slit my wrists or loaded the back of the pickup with fish guts and driven it over the spillway. He didn't push it but asked if he could bring his car over to Norm's station Saturday afternoon to wash it. We could talk then. I said sure.

"You guys coming up to the dance tonight?" he asked.

"Un-freaking-likely," I said. "Unless I decide to end it all."

We talked about the rest of the game a little and hung up. The whole incident didn't seem to bother him that much, and that bugged me. I wanted the whole world to be outraged, but especially Carter.

Becky didn't have much to say about the game. I jabbered a lot about injustice most of the way to Clear Lake, where we went bowling, but she spent most of the time teasing and flirting with me and generally making me feel good and taking my mind off it. It was nice to know that just because I wasn't a football star anymore, I didn't have to go back to being a dork. And as long as Becky was still with me, there was no way people would write me off completely. At least they'd have to wonder.

We bowled three or four games—I quit after she beat me—and went over to the local drive-in for a milk shake and some Tater Tots. We ran into a couple of guys from Clear Lake whose names I didn't know but who I recognized from football last year. They heard we'd won but didn't know any of the details.

"How's that black kid?" one of them asked.

"Good," I said, "and fast."

"He better than Cowans?"

I smiled. "He's so much better than Cowans it's indescribable. Boomer wouldn't be allowed to carry his worn-out sweaty jock from the locker room to the garbage can."

They looked at each other and back at me. "How about Sampson?"

"I don't know," I said. "Might be close."

They wanted to know more about him, like if he was mean or dirty or whatever. I told them his real name was Jackie Robinson, but they didn't get it. It sounded like maybe Lednecky coached at Clear Lake, too. I didn't tell them that Washington was probably on a slab in the morgue by then. I figured they ought to have to worry about him another day or so.

I started in again on the way home. I should have just shut up. It wasn't as big a thing when I was with Becky anyway because she never really cared that much about football and couldn't have cared less if I played. She was more concerned that I didn't get eaten up with it and become a terminal pain in the neck.

"You know about confrontation?" she said, scooting over close and laying her hand on my knee.

"Some, I suppose. What do you mean?"

"Well," she said, "when I lived back East, I used to go to a shrink."

"You mean a psychiatrist?" I interrupted. "You went to a psychiatrist?"

She nodded. "Actually he was just a psychologist. But I had to. It was the only way I could live with Mom. Talk about confrontations; we had confrontations like most people have lunch. Every day it was something. Every night I'd go to bed crying and swearing I'd never speak to her again, and the next day she'd bait me about something: grades, dates, not wearing makeup, wearing makeup, you name it. And finally she'd say the right thing, and away we'd go. I thought I was nuts. I mean, really crazy. None of it made sense, but I couldn't get out of it. I just couldn't understand why it worked the way it did."

"So what happened?"

"So I got an ax and chopped her up into little pieces and fed them to the neighbors' cat."

"Right," I said. "What happened?"

"Well," she said, "after I'd been going to Greg—he was my shrink—for about four months, he decided Mom was a certifiable loon, and he started working on me to let it go."

"What do you mean?"

"Just let it go," she said. "We sat there one day, and he had me identify all the warning signals, like 'You didn't wear that skirt with that blouse, did you?' or 'You know Jimmy won't respect you if you go to bed with him yet' or whatever. Then we decided when I saw one coming—and there were a million—I'd let it go. Not invest. Agree with her, space out, change the subject, pour myself a bowl of cornflakes, whatever. None of the confrontations were about things that were important to me anyway."

"So how'd it work?" I was sucked in.

"It drove her nuttier than she already was, but it let me off the hook. She and Daddy split up shortly after that, and I came with him, and that ended it."

"So what's this got to do with me and Lednecky?" I said. Nobody ever said I wasn't thick.

"Well, if you're anything like me, you're going to want to

defend your point with the rest of the kids at school when it comes up, which it will. You'll get all hot and end up going over and over it with your mom and dad and Carter and me and anyone who'll listen, at which point you will become a pain in the butt."

I had to admit that a few conversations had run through my mind already.

"But the truth is, the war's over. You did what you did and you were right and all the people who care about you are with you and you don't have to regurgitate this until June. It can be over if you want it to be."

I stared at the bright white lines shooting under the pickup and nodded slowly. It was worth thinking about. I sure needed some kind of plan for Monday. I wasn't looking forward to that at all.

"And another thing is," she said, "I don't want to waste my time with you on this. If you want, I'll quit cheerleading to show support. I just do it for exercise anyway. But I don't want us getting weighed down."

We decided there was no reason for her to quit cheerleading. If she did, she wouldn't be able to get out of school for away games.

She sure did seem grown-up.

When I dropped Becky off at her place, I felt pretty good. I hadn't absorbed all she said—I'm a pretty slow study—but I knew she was with me, and that's what it was really all about for me. I drove up to the reservoir, where the old highway that used to run to Modoc disappears into the water. It makes a natural loading and unloading ramp for water skiers and fishermen, and the city has widened it out and bordered it with small logs to make it accessible. I pulled into it and shut off the lights. The moon was more than three-quarters and lying low on the horizon, and I could see Ramsey's Peak silhouetted against the sky. The water was pretty calm, and the reflection of the moon bobbed and weaved lightly in the ripples.

I sat there contemplating Life After Football when the pickup cab lighted up, and I checked my rearview mirror to see a car pulling in behind me. I couldn't think of anyone I felt like talking to, so I cranked her up and turned around. It looked like the car was deliberately blocking me—kind of stuck there broadside between the logs that form the exit—and when I started to drive behind it, it backed up. I backed off and sat there, rolling down the window and straining to see who was inside. It looked like Mr. Williams's car, which meant Nancy Williams would be driving. She's a cheerleader, and she goes out with Boomer sometimes. I don't have to tell you that was a bad sign.

Sure enough, it was Nancy. She got out of the car and walked toward me with a beer in each hand. The drumbeat of my heart hammered out a clear message. It said: "This can't be good."

She held out one of the bottles. "Want a beer?" she asked.

"Hi, Nancy," I said. "Sure, why not?"

"Missed you at the dance."

I shrugged. Hell, she never danced with me anyway. Boomer would kill us both. Besides, she didn't like me.

"Can I get in?" she asked.

"What for?"

"Talk. I just want to talk with you for a while."

She was a little drunk, but not bad. I couldn't imagine what she might want to talk to me about.

"Who else is in the car?" I asked.

"Cindy and Carmen and Martha Shrivers."

"You just gonna let them sit there?"

"Unh-unh," she said. "They can take the car. You can take me home."

The faint odor of skunk.

"Tell you what," I said. "I ain't had a great day, and I think I'm just gonna go home and go to bed. I have to work tomorrow."

She turned and looked back toward her car and shrugged. The door opened, and who do you think stepped out but everyone's favorite fullback, Boomer Cowans.

I said, "Thanks, Nancy."

"Anytime."

Boomer had an open beer in his hand, and he staggered just a little. If he was really drunk, I had a chance to see sunrise.

He stopped at my window. "Well, well, well," he said, "if it ain't Trout's own silver rights worker sittin' right here, hustlin' my woman."

I didn't say anything, just looked straight ahead, trying to figure which end of the car I could get around.

"What's that crap you pulled today?" he said. "I had a good clean shot at that jungle bunny."

"Maybe I saw it wrong," I said.

"Maybe you're a worthless scumbag nigger lover."

I nodded. "Maybe that's it."

"I'm tired of your smart mouth!" he screamed, and lunged at the door. I heard a loud pop on the side of my head as his fist came through the open window, and I hit the starter as I quickly rolled up the window, trapping his arm between it and the top of the door. I shoved it into first and started toward the rear end of Nancy's car, figuring if I couldn't get around it, I'd knock it out of the way. Nancy was screaming at me and trying to get in to move it, and Boomer was still trying to hit me. My right side tires bounced over the log that borders the launch area, but I made it onto the highway okay and drove over close to the ditch. By then Boomer wasn't trying to hit me anymore; he was holding on for dear life. I lowered the window a little, pulled the door latch, and bashed into the door with my shoulder, sending him flying into the ditch. Then I pulled it shut and drove off. On the way home I remember thinking there must be some safe way to tell that dumb bastard that it isn't "silver" rights.

# CHAPTER 8

SATURDAY MORNING I got up early and was in and out of the Buckhorn by seven. That was way too early to run into Dakota. Then I went over and opened up the station. I was in the mood to keep busy, so I cleaned the place from top to bottom, even waxed the pop machine. About ten Carter pulled up around on the side and honked. Norm doesn't usually like a lot of kids hanging around and giving themselves free wash jobs and working on their cars or whatever because he says it looks "cruddy" and drives customers away. But Carter's different. He and Norm get along like buddies; Carter could probably pull right up in front of the pumps on the Fourth of July and wash his car, and Norm wouldn't care.

Anyway, we filled the wash bucket with soap and water, and I sat against the building where I could see the pumps while Carter washed.

He got right down to it. "You gonna try to get back on the team?"

I said, "Are you kidding?"

He raised his eyebrows and shrugged. "Hell of a lot of work down the drain."

Boy, he was right about that. There had been nights during the summer I'd gone down to the field after I closed the station at midnight to run wind sprints by myself and hit the blocking sled in the dark. Times when I'd been so psyched that making the team was all I could think of.

"Yeah, no lie," I said. "But I couldn't. I gotta live with myself, man. Besides, can you picture Lednecky letting me back on after yesterday?"

"He might," Carter said. "If you reached some kind of agreement and if the pressure was right."

For a second I visualized the agreement we'd come to. I laughed. "I can hear it now. 'Really, Coach, I lost my head, went completely crazy. Totally off my nut. Thought I heard you say you wanted Washington offed. I hear voices sometimes, you know. Please take me back. I'll pack Boomer's gear to away games and write all his English compositions for the rest of the semester so people will think he's literate. Okay, for the rest of the *year.*' No, I don't think so."

| 77

"It's up to you," Carter said. "I just hate to see you throw it all away. It's just that it kills me to set my sights on something and then not get it."

I was quiet for a minute. Carter and I were—still are—good friends, and I thought I knew him pretty well. But he hadn't said word one about what happened, and he didn't seem all that concerned with it. I was a little afraid to bring it up for fear it would put a rift between us, but damn it, he knew what had happened. So I went ahead.

"Shoot, Cart. I watched that being set up all week. So did you. I mean, how can you play for him? Hell, who knows, we probably would have won that game yesterday anyway, but doing it like that, I don't know, it's like losing. I just can't go along with it."

He stopped soaping the hood. "I don't play for Lednecky, Louie. I play for me. And you guys. Lednecky's small-time. He's got no class. His whole act stinks. But it's going to be tough to get a scholarship to play anywhere as it is. If I quit, there's no chance. I like football, and I want to play in college. I'm not going to throw it away because my coach is a lowlife."

I hate it. The bastard made sense. He always makes sense. How come everybody always makes sense but me?

"Yeah," I said, "but it seems like there's a 'point of honor' in there somewhere, at least for me."

"Maybe there should be for me, too," he said, "but it would be pretty futile. I could quit and maybe wreck his winning season and all that, but where would it end? I mean, I hate to say it, but there aren't too many people in this town who would side with us against an undefeated football coach. Not many people would believe that whole thing was intentional, or care. If they did, they'd blame it on Boomer, not Lednecky."

He was probably right. I felt my righteous mission crumbling a little.

"And let me tell you something else, buddy," he said. "You ask around and you'd think there was no prejudice against blacks in this town. You know why that is? It's because there aren't any blacks. If we had a lot of different races, we'd get our share just like anyplace else. So I don't think you could generate a lot of sympathy for Washington." He looked off across the street for a second. "But God, Louie, he was good."

He was using the chamois to dry off the car. "Look, buddy, this is it," he said. "Last year in high school; the end of a whole part of our lives. I don't even know whether that's a big deal or not, but it won't hurt to make the most of it. I'm going to play ball one way or the other, but I'd like it a hell of a lot more if you were there. Think about it. If you decide to try to get back on, I can help. If not, that's okay, too."

The thing I hate about life, so far, is that nothing's ever clear. Every time you get things all figured out, somebody throws in another kink.

I said I'd think about it. Besides the piles and piles of compost I'd have to eat for Lednecky, there was one other concern. If I walked onto the same practice field with Boomer Cowans, no doctor in his right mind would give me more than twenty-four hours to live.

I told Carter what happened the night before up at the lake.

He shook his head. "I suppose before this year is over, Boomer and I'll have to tangle," he said. "It's been coming for a long time." He put his head down, then looked up at me. "If he touches you, he won't touch the ball again all season, whether you come back or not. We can win without him. He'll be making his living as a blocker."

It's funny. By the time Carter left I was actually thinking about trying to get back on. So much for principles and right and wrong and all that. The truth was I really had invested a lot, and the idea of being a jerk in everyone's eyes wasn't all that appealing. It's a shame what can happen to your resolve.

I spent the rest of Saturday being a real pain in the butt to Norm and Brenda and Becky, trying to get them to talk me into getting back on the team. None of them would.

Sunday morning I was down cleaning out the Buckhorn, and Dakota came in. He came right out and asked me what had happened, and I told him. By the time I was finished I was convinced I'd done the right thing again.

"You do what you gotta do," was about all he said.

Monday I came to school later than usual and got there just in time to slide into my seat in English class as the bell rang. There wasn't a cross burned on my desk or a strangled cat inside, so I figured Carter had talked to Boomer already.

I'm pretty sure the whole student body didn't get together and vote me out of existence, but if I hadn't hunted up Becky or Carter, I could have easily gone through the whole day without having a single conversation.

By lunchtime I was starting to feel invisible. Carter and Becky and I decided to go down to the Chief for a cheeseburger.

"I talked to Lednecky," Carter said. "Just feelin' him out. He didn't make any promises, but I think if you said the right things, you could get back on. He was kind of a bastard, but I got the feeling he'd like to see the whole thing drop. Won't hurt to see, if you want to."

I still couldn't make up my mind. "I don't know," I said. "I don't know if I'm up for that kind of abuse."

"Well, you better decide," he said. "It may be a one-day offer. Hell, just go see him during study hall. What can it hurt?"

Crap like that is easy for Carter to say and do. I mean, he really isn't afraid of Lednecky. He'll walk in and meet him man-to-bastard anytime. But the bastard scares me to death. He gets you on his turf, and you can't come away feeling any way but bad.

I didn't have to decide whether or not to look him up. When we got back to school, there was a notice on the hall bulletin board telling me to report to the office during the next period. It was signed by Mr. Jasper. Now there's a name that fits. Like I said before, he's the superintendent and principal of the high school.

When I walked into the outer office, the secretary, Mrs. Roundy, told me to go in, that they were waiting for me. I said, "I'll bet," and she smiled. I went in.

Jasper was standing behind his desk, with Lednecky sitting to his right. Basically Jasper's just an older version of Lednecky. In fact, he used to coach, which is, as I understand it, a prerequisite for getting into high school administration. Jasper's scarier, though. He's had longer to work on his act, and he's smarter.

"Have a seat, Louie," he said.

I sat, facing them both.

"Coach Lednecky and I have been having quite a discussion about you," he said.

I sort of nodded and cleared my throat.

"The first thing I'd like to do here is get your version of what happened last Friday. That was quite a display you put on. I have to admit I'm pretty appalled at your language."

I tried to remember what I'd said.

There was silence.

"Well?"

I decided I wanted to play football. "Well, I guess I thought Boomer tried to injure Washington on purpose," I said.

"Is that all?"

"Well, I guess I thought Coach Lednecky put him up to it."

"What gave you that idea?" he asked.

"I don't know," I said, beginning the sellout statement of the century. "Probably a mistake I made from some of the pregame psyche-up stuff. I don't know. I guess I get pretty excited sometimes." I felt a tremendous flood of anxiety that, as I look back on it, was probably a combination of excitement about getting back on the team, self-contempt for what I was saying, and fear. Mostly fear. A little trickle of sweat ran down from both armpits toward my brand-new Jockey shorts.

Lednecky looked me square in the eye. "That's not the way we play football here at Trout," he lied. "I may coach rough football, but I coach clean football."

I nodded. "Yes, sir," I said quietly.

Jasper interrupted. "I understand you'd like to get back on the team, Louie."

I nodded again. "Yes, sir. I mean, I don't know. I mean, I think so."

"You *think* so?"

"I mean—"

Lednecky cut in. "You better *know* so, Banks. Carter came to me this morning and said you two had talked things out. Believe me, after the stunt you pulled on Friday, I had no reason whatsoever to even consider taking you back. But Carter convinced me to talk with you. I like to give a boy a chance to make amends for his mistakes, but so far I'm not impressed. You should be on your knees."

I decided I didn't want to play football.

He went on. "I have a tremendous reservation about letting you back. I won't have you running around with that attitude, contaminating my football team." He stood up and walked to the other side of the office. "These are my conditions," he said. "Take them or leave them. You make a full apology to the team in a meeting before practice today. You write an apology to the school that will be published in the school paper. You run the mile for time before every practice for two weeks, and you start back on the third string and work your way up."

My guts churned. I looked to Jasper.

He nodded. "Well, what do you say?"

I gave it up. Just let it go, like Becky said. And I wasn't scared anymore. "Naw," I said, "I don't think so. It's not worth it. Not even close."

Lednecky started to walk out.

"Wait a minute, Coach," Jasper said. He turned back to me. "I want to get this taken care of once and for all. What do you think would be fair, Louie? I'm interested."

I cleared my throat. "Well, first, I'm not willing to start back on third string. And I can't see starting every practice with a timed mile. Maybe for track, but not football. Then I think Coach Lednecky should submit a written apology to Washington to the *Daily Statesman* down in Boise. And maybe during the meeting he scheduled for me today, he could apologize to the team for teaching us dirty football. And we could start the whole thing off by having him apologize to you right now for not telling the truth about what happened."

I may be a wussy most of the time, but I have my moments.

"That's enough!" Jasper yelled. He caught himself. "Are you calling Coach Lednecky a liar?"

"I'm not calling Coach Lednecky anything," I said. "I'm saying that what he's telling you about the game on Friday isn't true."

84

Jasper, smart as he is, couldn't make the distinction. He pointed a finger at me. "Louie, you're about to get yourself in a lot of trouble."

"Then maybe I should go back to class," I said.

We stared at each other.

"Louie," he said, "you're suspended until further notice. I will not have this kind of insolence going on in my school."

I stood up. "Okay," I said. "I'll get my stuff."

# CHAPTER 9

WHEN I TOLD BECKY later about the conversation in Jasper's office, she said she was proud of me. And to tell you the truth, I was feeling pretty proud of myself. I came out of the office seeing things completely differently from the way I had going in. And I didn't have to worry about the math test I was supposed to take that afternoon, having been given the old boot.

Anyway, the bell rang just as I was coming out, and Becky met me at the lockers, where I was clearing out some of my stuff. I didn't take it all because I knew I'd be back.

"Suspended? They suspended you?" she said. "I don't believe it!"

"Go ask," I said.

"I believe *you*," she said, "I just don't believe *it*." She was ready to go in and unload on them. Right then. To tell you the truth, if she had, I don't think they'd have stood a chance, but I told her to hold off and we'd talk about it later.

Then Carter came up. "How'd it go?" he asked.

I said not quite as planned. "Gave me the boot. Good luck on the math test. Try to remember the answers. I'll be back."

He said we'd work something out, that he'd talk to me after practice.

I really wasn't too worried about whether or not I'd get back in school. I mean, I don't think they can expel you forever when there's no place else to go, especially if you're not armed and dangerous. Besides, Norm's the chairman of the school board, and though he doesn't usually exercise much muscle about daily goings-on in school, I figured Jasper wouldn't be comfortable letting too many board meetings go by with me out. And he'd have to meet with Norm and Brenda as parents. That's the rule when someone gets suspended. Since I'd been pretty cool in the office and hadn't done some dumb-butt thing that Norm couldn't defend, and since Norm's a lot smarter than Jasper, I figured my days as an outcast were numbered.

When I talked to Becky that night, she said if I thought it would do any good, she'd quit cheerleading and raise a stink, that this whole thing was getting too crazy. Like she'd said before, she just did it for exercise anyway. I said that didn't seem necessary; it *was* good exercise, and I kind of liked going out with a cheerleader. We have girls' sports at Trout, now that there's a law, but they aren't taken very seriously because Jasper and Lednecky, who are the powers around here, think that a girls' sports program is nonsense. In fact, back in the days when Jasper and I were still talking to each other and I was doing an article on girls' sports for the school paper, he said he couldn't get behind an athletic program for girls because girls weren't emotionally equipped for competitive athletics. That was just a fact of life. Too many tears. I heard Lednecky say one time that Trout was shooting for minimum compliance with the law: Let some teacher make a few extra bucks coaching the girls, give them gym time when it didn't interfere with the boys, and let them have their fun. Girls' athletics has come a little ways here since then mostly because of some girls' parents pointing out the finer points of that law, but all in all, it's a pretty sad program, not one Becky would have ever been interested in getting into.

If it wasn't being done well—whatever it was—Becky wouldn't do it.

Jasper and Lednecky are pretty cute talking about people's emotional equipment. Last year at the district basketball tournament we lost the championship game to Modoc, and Boomer tore out a whole section of lockers. Ripped 'em right off the wall. Then he went back up to the gym and threatened their high scorer. That's not what I'd call emotionally equipped; that's emotionally armed. When the dust had cleared, Trout paid for the lockers and Boomer was on "probation," even though basketball season was over and there was nothing to be on probation about. Jasper and Lednecky both said that though they thought Boomer took it too far, they were glad to see he had such a competitive spirit. Christ, Justice isn't only blind; she's deaf and dumb.

After I took Becky home, Carter called to get the hot poop. I told him what happened in the office, and he said he didn't blame me and that maybe he'd misread Lednecky. He asked if there was anything he could do and I told him not to forget the answers to that math test, that I'd be back in a week or so.

I spent some long mornings down at the Buckhorn for the next week. I'd clean up and Dakota would come down and we'd shoot a few games of pool and talk. I probably learned more in that one week than I'd learned in four years of school. And he showed me a thing or two about pool.

I remember one morning after he'd beaten me three games in a row—and remember, one of his hands is a *hook*—he put his cue back up in the rack and asked me what I was going to do with my life.

I said I was going to wait for them to let me back in school, then just keep my mouth shut and graduate and get out of here.

He hoisted himself up on the bar like he does and said, "You know, it's a funny thing. You get holed up in a little pissant town like this and you don't get away much and you start to think the way things are here is the way things are. It ain't necessarily so."

I said I didn't know what he meant.

"Well," he said, "take this whole football deal and you gettin' kicked out of school an' all."

"What about it?"

"Up to a few days ago they had you thinkin' the most important damn thing in the world was playin' football. Told me so yourself. Now they got you thinkin' the most important thing in the world is goin' back to school—on their terms—an' graduatin'. All that's goin' on there is them tellin' you what's important. Sounds to me like they don't know their butt from what's important."

I started to interrupt.

"Hold on a minute," he said. "From what you've told me, Lednecky gave that colored kid a raw deal an' you took a righteous stand. Now to my way of thinkin' it's a damn shame to back off a righteous stand, which you almost did the other day in the office, or you wouldn't have been there. A man has to plant his feet somewhere an' say, 'This is as far as I go an' anyone tries to push me any farther's gonna have his hands full.'"

I just looked at him. Not too much to argue with there. Finally I said, "Yeah, well, what now?"

"Hell," he said, "I don't know." He raised his hook. "I'm just a dern fool pirate never got outta the third grade. What's next is up to you. But damn it, there's other places you can go to school. Clear Lake's only a half hour up the road. Or you could go down to the big city and graduate outta Boise or Borah. Hell, I'd grubstake that, an' so would your ol' man, I bet. I'm sayin' you don't have to go up there on your knees to get back in school."

I promised I wouldn't get on my knees to get back in. The idea of driving to Clear Lake wasn't a bad one. It might be tougher in the winter, but certainly possible. I didn't want to go to Boise or Borah, though, because that would mean I'd have to live down there and I didn't want to leave Becky.

While I was racking up the balls and thinking about that, there was a knock at the back door, so I went to open it. It was Mrs. Esau in her black skirt and her black blouse and her black hat and her Bible, which was also black.

She said, "Why, Louie Banks, why in heaven's name aren't you in school?" but didn't stop for an answer. She brushed right past me to the bar, where Dakota was sitting.

"I don't suppose you have time to talk with me today either, Dakota," she said.

Dakota let out kind of a long sigh, like he'd been trapped, and said, "Sure, Marionette. Got all the time in the world."

Mrs. Esau's a widow, and she spends about eight hours a day going around to people's houses and businesses to see if they've been saved. Norm says she's on a pension and doesn't have anything better to do with her time. The best way to get rid of her is to say yes, you have been saved and Lord praise her for her good work; but most people don't think of that, and they try all kinds of things to shake her. Trying to shake her is the best way to keep her around.

"You know I don't take to churchgoin', Marionette," Dakota said, "so don't start with me. As to whether I've been saved or not, well, I'm not sure I'm drownin'."

"Well, you are, son," she said. "Drowning in a sea of your own sins."

"Yeah," he said. "I reckon there's plenty of them, but first off I'm three years older than you, so don't go callin' me son. An' second, I got a couple a questions."

She smiled. "I'll answer them if I can."

"Okay. Now you say God perty much knows everything. He knows what you done an' what you're gonna do."

"That's correct."

"An' He's runnin' things, right? I mean if He wants to, He can make things go His way."

"Things do go His way."

You could see he was setting her up, but she couldn't.

"So I guess He's pretty hot stuff. Nobody gets over on Him. 'Shapes the destinies of nations,' I think is how you put it last time."

"Yes, I did say that." She seemed pleased. "What's your question, Dakota?"

"Well," Dakota said, "He knows everything, He goes where He wants, probably eats out at the finest restaurants, rubs shoulders with presidents and kings. Why do ya s'pose He needs a crippled ol' duff like me kissin' His butt? I'm here doin' my best; why does He keep siccin' you on me? I like to think He has a little more class than that."

92

The conversation went on from there, but I was about to crack up, so I excused myself and headed for the station.

The next day I was cleaning up the bar—Dakota was still upstairs in bed—when I heard another knock at the back door. I thought about not answering it because I didn't want to be stuck in the bar with Mrs. Esau and no Dakota to protect me, but then I heard a man's voice calling through it to me, so I opened it. It was Coach Madison.

"Thought I'd find you here," he said as he closed the door behind him.

"What're you doing here?" I asked. "Aren't you supposed to be in school?"

He walked over and racked up the balls. "It's my prep period," he said. "I told 'em I had to go to the bank."

I nodded. No way I could figure why he was there.

"You play?" he said, nodding at the table.

"There's a running debate about it," I said.

"Break."

I broke, and nothing went in. Coach started picking off the solids while he talked. "Louie, I can't say this publicly—I don't have that much clout around here—but I have to say I support what you did last Friday and I respect you for doing it. I'll do whatever I can to help you get back in school."

I have to admit I was pretty shocked. I mean, I always thought Madison was a pretty square guy, but he was a coach.

"Really," I said. "Geez, thanks. I mean, that's really nice

to know." I think I was a little embarrassed. So was he.

"Coach and I have had some conversations about it," he said, "some of them pretty hot. The bottom line is, if I raise hell, I'm out just like you are. That's not real good on a rookie coach's record."

I started to say that's okay, but he kept going. "I won't coach under him again; I'll leave if I have to. Football's a good sport. There really are some good things to learn from it, but not that way."

I got a couple of turns before he sank all the solids and went after the eight ball, which he dropped on the first shot. He laid the cue on the table. "Gotta get back. You hang in there."

"Listen," I said, "it's enough just knowing there's someone up there besides Becky and Carter who doesn't want my butt nailed to the goalposts. Thanks."

He left out the back way.

I'm such a rotten pool player.


Actually the meeting with Jasper and Norm and Brenda was pretty uneventful, but it was interesting. It was Friday afternoon, and the team was playing at Bear Creek. Unless you can get a ride to the game with somebody responsible, you have to stay in school for away games and have regular classes if you're not a player or a cheerleader. Bear Creek's quite a ways, and they're not very good, so not many people went. We walked into school just as the bell rang between sixth and seventh periods, so I ran into a lot of kids. Nobody said much.

Norm and Brenda and I had decided they should do the talking. We'd talked the whole thing right into the ground and were solid in our position. Norm thought Jasper could hear it better from them. That was fine with me; I'd said all I had to say.

We walked in and everyone shook hands and it was all kind of formal and uncomfortable. Jasper looked as uncomfortable as anyone, and that made me feel good.

Norm got right down to it. "Well, Tony," he said, "what has to be done here?"

"I'm not sure, Norm. Louie's gotten himself into some pretty hot water."

"How do you mean?"

"Well," Jasper said, "you saw him at the game Friday. And he was pretty insolent with Coach Lednecky and me earlier this week. We both agreed we can't have Louie running loose in our school with that kind of attitude."

Norm nodded and scratched his chin. "Tell you what, Tony. I've listened to Louie's story, and whether or not he was right in what he did, he thought he was. Now we could argue all afternoon about what was said, and perspectives and all that, but it wouldn't do any good, so here's my proposal. If you're prepared to take him back, Brenda and I have his assurance that his intent is to follow the rules and graduate. Louie's never been a problem, and we feel we can trust his word."

Boy, my dad's an articulate bastard when he wants to be.

"If you're not prepared to take him back," he went on, "then Brenda and I will have to act on that. I'm not sure what that means. We'll cross that one if we come to it."

I wasn't sure, but I thought it sounded a little like a threat.

Jasper leaned back in his chair. "Norm, don't you think an apology is in order here?"

"An apology for what?"

"For his behavior out there on the field last week," Jasper said, "and for his little display here in the office."

Norm was quiet again. He looked at Brenda, then at me. Finally he said, "Quite honestly, no, I don't."

Jasper looked a little shocked, but you had to be quick to catch it. "Would you mind telling me why you feel that way?" he said.

"Because he isn't sorry. Asking him to apologize would be asking him to lie, and that's not my way."

Silence again. And Norm was in complete control of it. Finally Jasper said, "There's one condition."

"Which is?"

"Louie can't participate in any interscholastic activities as long as he's at Trout."

"I'll have to think about that," Norm said.

For the first time I spoke up. "That's okay, Norm. I'm not going out for any more sports. All I want to do is do my work and get out."

Norm nodded, but he turned back to Jasper. "I understand that, but I'm still not sure I'm willing to make that concession."

They talked about it for another half hour or so, with Jasper saying he thought there had to be some public show of punishment—that my kind of attitude could be damaging to the whole school—and Norm defending my right to stand on principle. They didn't make a final decision but agreed to deal with it if it came up. I was sure it wouldn't.

When we walked out, Norm said, "Louie, *never* give anyone anything you don't have to in these kinds of negotiations."

"It didn't seem like a big deal," I said. "I'm not going out for anything."

"Then don't give it up on principle," he said. "It's like an admission. Beside, you don't know what you'll want to do come spring. You may want to run track. And if you do, you have the right. Always leave your options open. Whatever you do, leave your options."

The point was well taken, but I couldn't see myself closing out my high school career running around in circles and then throwing up.

# CHAPTER 10

THAT NIGHT after dinner I was pretty much at loose ends. Norm didn't need me down at the station; he had bookwork to do down there, and there wouldn't be enough business to keep both of us busy. The team wouldn't be getting back from Bear Creek until late, so I couldn't see Becky until Saturday.

I decided to take the pickup out for a little spin and try out the new cassette deck I'd installed during my suspension from school. I got a Waylon Jennings tape out of the glove compartment, cranked her up real loud, and headed west out of town. The pickup was running smooth, the tape deck worked like standard equipment, and I was feelin' good, bouncing around in the seat, singing "Good Hearted Woman," and thinking about my life.

Before I knew it, I passed a sign that said "Salmon River—31 miles" and decided why not. In a little more than half an hour I pulled up in front of the Seven Devils' Café.

Salmon River had played at home that day, so the place was humming. A lot of kids were in the Seven Devils, and the drive-in down the block was packed. It had been almost an hour since dinner, so I decided to go in and have a burger. A few guys looked up when I came in, but if anyone recognized me, they didn't come over. I sat at the counter and ordered. In the back at a long table a bunch of Salmon River players sat eating burgers and shakes and screwing around. Washington was with them; in fact, he seemed to be the center of attention, telling stories and, at one point, twirling his hamburger around on one finger like a basketball. He couldn't be *that* great an athlete; he lost the meat.

I wanted to go over and ask how he was doing, but to tell the truth, I was a little afraid to. I'm not sure why; I mean, I didn't think they'd jump me or anything. Once, when Washington got up to go to the can, I could see that his ribs were bound tightly and he moved real slow and carefully. But he still moved like a jock.

Just as I was getting ready to leave, Sally Larson, who used to live in Trout, came through the door with a couple of girl friends. The Larsons moved to Salmon River when it became clear that Trout wasn't going to spend much serious energy on girls' sports. Mr. Larson just applied for the same job he had in our mill in theirs. Sally's probably one of the best athletes we ever had in that town, right up there with Carter and Boomer. Played Little League up through Ponies and went to all kinds of girls' sports camps in the summers. She's tall and lean and eats like a horse and is really pretty. I had a horrible crush on her in fourth grade. She beat me up about once a week that year. We got to be pretty good friends in junior high, and we still made it a point to say hi anytime our schools played each other.

She ran over and gave me a big hug. "What're you doing over here?" she said. "I thought you guys played Creek today."

I told her I was out of the violent world of football.

"How come?" she said. "Was it over Kevin getting hurt? We couldn't tell what was going on from the sideline last week, but you looked pretty crazy out there."

I smiled and nodded. "I guess I *was* pretty crazy out there."

We sat down in a booth, and she introduced me to her friends, and they all ordered burgers. I figured I could do with another chocolate milk shake, so I ordered again.

"So did you quit or get thrown off?" she asked.

"I have a feeling that depends on who's telling the story," I said. "I quit. Listen, that black kid over there is Washington, isn't he?"

She nodded. "Want to meet him?"

"No, that's okay. Good to see he's still alive, though."

"He's supposed to be back out in a couple of weeks," she said, "soon as his bruised ribs heal."

I almost felt let-down. My sacrifice had been for a couple of bruised ribs. Washington wasn't dead or anything. In a couple of weeks he'd be back playing ball like nothing happened. "So what did everyone up here think about how he got hurt?" I asked.

The burgers came, and Sally took a big bite out of hers and said, "They were pretty ticked off, but everybody knows Boomer Cowans. You don't want to let him get a shot at you."

I said, "Boy, don't I know that." I started to tell her how Lednecky had set it all up, but then I thought of how Becky said I'd want to keep hashing and rehashing it, so I let it go.

"How's he get along here?" I asked.

Sally took another bite—about half the burger—and said, "Great. Everybody loves him. He's funny and smart, and you've seen what kind of athlete he is. He came up last summer from Oakland, California, because his parents thought he was getting in with a bad crowd. Drugs and stuff."

"What's he say about that?"

"That he was getting in with a bad crowd. Drugs and stuff. Started ripping folks off; all that big-city crap. Says he's glad he's here."

"Does he take any crap for being black?" It was hard to figure how we'd gotten up so much hate for him at Trout when Sally made it sound like he was getting the key to the city in Salmon River.

"He doesn't take much crap for anything." She stuffed the rest of the burger in her mouth. "You hear some things behind his back, but never to his face. I don't even think he knows it's going on. If he does, it doesn't seem to bother him."

I sat there quietly for a minute, watching the guys at the back table and wondering how Sally had perfected the art of stuffing her mouth to capacity and still articulating like she was in a debate tournament. I mean, she could take that act on the road.

I stayed a little longer; we asked about each other's folks and talked about our plans after school. Then I said I ought to be getting back to Trout. Sally gave me another big hug and said she'd get my shake. I thanked her and headed for the pickup.

Driving home, I wished I'd have let her introduce me to those guys, especially Washington. I felt like I had some kind of special connection to him. Besides that, I just wanted to sit at the table, be part of what I'd worked all summer and fall for. That was a part of my life that was gone before I even had a good taste of it.

What the hell, I had Becky.

# CHAPTER 11

MOST PEOPLE around Trout who drive pickups—
which is most people around Trout—have gun racks behind the seat, and the bulk of those racks have loaded
guns in them. I guess a lot of people around here like to
kill things. You get a lot of "accidents" due to that. You'd
be surprised at the number of times, just in my lifetime,
that two guys who didn't particularly care for each other
went out deer hunting and only one came back. Pleading
"I thought he was a deer" around here is a lot like pleading "temporary insanity" in other places. And every once
in a while one of those guns will "accidentally" go off dur-

ing cleaning and kill some guy who's been sleeping with the gun cleaner's wife. Guys clean their guns in the strangest places.

Anyway, I've got a gun rack in my Chevy, too, but I don't carry a gun in it. Guns scare me. I carry a huge pepperoni I got down at Smoky Joe's just outside Boise. Had it custom-made. If I'm ever caught in a blizzard, I may freeze to death, but I sure as hell won't starve. It would take me three years to eat that thing. I've had it almost eight months, and though it's getting pretty hard, it's still good. Smoky Joe said it would live longer than I would.

Once it almost got me beat up. Guess who. Right. Boomer asked me why I had it, and when I explained it was my survival kit, he said bullshit, it was because I was too yellow to carry a gun, that I was always doing stupid things to cover up what a wussy I was. When I told him the sheriff made me check my shootin' iron at the jail when I came into this tinhorn town, he came after me. Did I say the guy's got no sense of humor? Luckily Carter was around.

Later Carter told me we might have to load up my pepperoni one of these days and hunt that bastard down like a dirty dog. There've been times when that didn't sound like such a bad idea, but it's so big I'd be afraid to shoot it.

Life was pretty uneventful for me through the rest of football season and into the winter. The hardest part was not going to the games. I really wanted to watch Carter and some of the other guys—they were tearing up the league—but I just couldn't stand to be there and not get in on it. So I'd deliver stove oil for Norm or let myself into the Buckhorn to shoot pool and feel sorry for myself. As much pool as I played, you'd think I'd have gotten better. The season ended just as predicted. Trout won the league, with Salmon River finishing second, and went on to win one more state championship. Washington came back in a couple of weeks, like Sally said, and ran up some pretty fair statistics. There were still times when I wished he'd been put out for the season, to make what I'd done seem worth it, but mostly I was glad he was okay. Oh, yeah, and they named the gym after Lednecky. We're the only school in the league whose gymnasium has a name. They even put some of those gold letters above the entrance. Somehow some of them keep mysteriously disappearing, so it says EDNECK or LED ECK or something weird. They just can't seem to keep them up there. Must be using the wrong kind of glue.

I couldn't turn out for basketball, which was fine with me. Jasper went ahead and told everybody that I'd been suspended from further interscholastic activities—fairly quietly, I noticed—and I didn't say anything to Norm about it because I didn't want to raise another stink. I play basketball a lot like I play pool and turned out before only because everyone else did and it was a way to keep in shape. Lednecky's the head basketball coach, too, so even if I had fought the ruling, I'd never have played a minute in a game. Not being allowed to turn out just took the pressure off.

My relationship with Becky grew more and more amazing. We got closer and closer, and the underlying fear that she was suddenly going to come to her senses and drop me like a hot rock disappeared. After one of the record dances at the school we almost had sex, and it was pretty clear to both of us that it was going to happen. In fact, I did have sex after that dance, but only my undershorts knew for sure. Becky said she wasn't up for making love in the front seat of a pickup in the company of a giant pepperoni. Seemed like pretty heavy competition to me, too.

But it was moving right along.

Carter and I still found time for each other, too. I don't know what I'd have done without him. He kept me feeling okay about myself without the help of sports. That's hard to do. It was like having Clint Eastwood or Kojak or somebody like you. I didn't have to prove anything to him.

Still, I wasn't a favorite among the masses, and there weren't many teachers I'd have felt comfortable asking for a letter of recommendation from. Unless I wanted to go to college in El Salvador or Iran or someplace.

Snow came early this year, like the *Farmer's Almanac* said it would. Sometimes you don't get it until right around Christmas, but this year the trick-or-treaters were decked out in their snow boots, trudging through two or three inches of it and killing each other with snowballs. It was a long, hard winter, weather-wise.

I started cross-country skiing in early November, mostly by accident. I was cleaning out my grandmother's barn when I ran across this really long pair of wooden skis with nothing but toe straps for bindings. They looked ripe for firewood until my grandmother told me what they were. She said my granddad used to go out for three or four days at a time on them when he was still alive. Survival trips, he called them, and they must have been just that, from what she told me. He came to Trout when it was being settled, and when there got to be about five hundred people, he felt it was getting too big. So he'd head for the hills and try to live like the Indians did in their time. 'Course they didn't have cross-country skis, but then he didn't have as much time to spend in the woods as they did. He'd take a little food just in case; but he hunted with a bow and slept in lean-tos made of branches, and Grandma said she never remembered him having to eat any of the food he took. He never killed more than he could eat, and he had a lot of respect for the country and the animals that lived there, and she wished he'd lived until I was older—long enough to pass that on to me.

I promised her I'd never kill more than I could eat.

Anyway, the skis intrigued me, so I decided to give them a try. They were every bit as unmanageable as they looked, especially with only the leather toe strap to keep your foot in. Dakota informed me, however, that if I'd bother to look around me—at the cross-country skiing boom—I'd see a lot of advances had been made since 1915, so I drove down to Boise to get something a little more modern. I'd saved plenty of money, so I had no trouble setting myself up with all the finest gear.

There really isn't much to it once you get the hang of making it up the steep hills, and by the middle of November I was spending most of the time I wasn't working or with Becky whipping through the hills around Trout.

Naturally it proved to Boomer that I was as big a wussy as he'd always said I was because if I had a hair anywhere on my body, I'd be learning to jump, like he would be if basketball practice hadn't already started.

Carter rented some stuff and went out with me once, but it didn't take long for us to figure out it wasn't the sport for him. Man was meant to move his athletics indoors when the snow flies, he said. The Good Lord couldn't respect a man who would deliberately go out and freeze his butt when he could be in by a warm fire. The Good Lord appreciated intelligence.

Becky went out with me a few times after school, and she liked it a lot. She didn't have as much time to play around with it, though, because she had music to play and grades to get and more damn irons in the fire than you'd need to brand every cow in your herd with a different brand each. She was always taking a test for some kind of scholarship or some highfallutin summer program being offered to high school geniuses by some highfallutin university like Stanford, which is down in California, close to San Francisco, I think.

It was because of cross-country skiing and because part of the roof of Lednecky Gym caved in from the weight of the snow that Becky and I finally got a chance to be really alone together. Actually it was because we were both horny, but those things got us to the right place and time.

After the first couple of times we'd gone skiing, Becky decided that when the snow got really deep, we should ski out to their cabin, which is a summer place a few miles off the Warm Lake road that you can't get to by car in the winter because the county doesn't plow it out. We could drive to the turnoff and ski the last five or six miles. Imagine the number of trips to the bathroom I made thinking about that.

Luckily no one was in the gym when it caved in or they'd have gotten several tons of snow and wood down on them. It just happened there were no PE classes scheduled for that period. Most of the seniors were in the study hall practicing a skit for the Junior-Senior Variety Show that was supposed to be the next night. We heard this big boom and all went hauling out to see what had happened. Mark Robeson took one look and said, "Who'd have thought the Russians would pick Trout High School to demonstrate their first strike capability?" That's about what it looked like. I was standing right under "LEDNECKY" and looked up and said, "It couldn't have happened to a nicer gym," only to turn around and see the Legend after which it was named standing right behind me. I want to tell you there was a pretty uneasy silence there for a minute.

Anyway, by the time last period had started, we were informed that the basketball game that night and the variety show the next night would be postponed indefinitely, so the weekend was free for both of us. Becky caught up with me at the lockers after school and jabbed me in the ribs. "Hey, big boy," she said in her best Mae West, "want some candy?"

"Huh?"

"Wanna come out to my place this weekend?"

"The cabin?"

"The cabin."

She didn't have any trouble getting permission; she'd already told her dad she was considering going out, though she didn't say I'd be coming along. He didn't ask, but I'm sure he knew. He figured she could take care of herself, which was good thinking. I wasn't so sure Norm and Brenda would be ready to let me hike out into the wilderness to lose my innocence, but I figured if I started with Norm, it might not have to go any farther.

I walked into his office, palms sweating, and asked for the weekend off.

"Sure," he said. "I think I ought to be able to handle it. What've you got in mind?"

"Skiing out to Becky's summer place," I said.

"Alone?"

"Not exactly."

"You're either alone or you're not alone," he said. "You're not 'not exactly' alone. Is Becky going?"

I nodded.

"Does her dad know?"

"He knows she's going," I said.

He nodded and thought for a minute. "You know what you're doing?"

I shrugged. "Yeah, I think so." I didn't have a clue.

He kind of relaxed and leaned back in his chair, propping his feet up on the desk. "What're you going to tell your mother?"

I flinched a little. It wouldn't be as easy with her as it was with Norm. Not even close. "I thought we might say I was going down to Boise to get those parts for the meter on the truck," I said. "And staying overnight."

"You mean lie?"

I thought for a second. "Yeah, lie," I said.

"And you want to drag me into it?"

"It would sure make it a whole lot easier."

He made a tent with his fingers below his chin and stared at me.

"Besides," I said, sort of smiling, "why would we want to drag her into this sordid mess? She'd only be mad—or disappointed."

"You've got a point there," he said, looking at the ceiling. "Christ, my kid's got me lying to my wife. It's starting. Your grandmother always warned me I'd have kids of my own someday."

I couldn't believe he was really going to do it. But we talked awhile longer, and he decided there was no reason to make a big deal out of it. Even though it was the biggest deal of my life, to date, I agreed. We worked it out so he would say he was sending me for parts. Then I would call from there and say I had to wait till early Sunday morning to get them. Of course, he would get the call.

I left early Saturday morning to pick up Becky—before Brenda was up to see me headed for Boise, where there was no snow, with my skis. We stopped at the Chief and had a stack of pancakes with some of the old codgers who get up that early and listened to them talk about the Russians and whether the mill would lay off any more men and who the idiot was that didn't have the snow shoveled off the roof of the gym. Then we headed out.

I was pretty quiet most of the way to the turnoff, really having a hard time thinking of what to say. Becky didn't say much either, just sat close with her hand on my knee.

Finally, just before we got to the turnoff, I said, "Are you sure about this?"

She punched me in the ribs. "What's the matter? Chicken?"

I nodded. "Yup. I'd say that's a good description of what I am."

She squeezed my knee and said, "Don't worry about it."

"Right."

She asked how I'd gotten permission.

"You wouldn't believe it," I said. "Norm's crazy. He acts like he's sending me out on a dangerous mission. He's keeping it quiet, though." I told her about the proposed trip to Boise.

"Maybe he is sending you out on a dangerous mission," she said. "Ever think of that?"

"Maybe he is. Hope I come back with the goods."

There was a little silence. "Actually the only danger is to Norm," I said. "If Brenda finds out he lied to her, his life ain't worth a plugged nickel."

When we got to the turnoff, I turned the pickup around and got it as close in to the edge of the road as I could and unloaded the skis and packs. We threw everything over the snowbank, which was about as high as the cab, and put on our skis sitting on top of it. As we got away from the road, the weekend took a turn for the amazing. The sky was overcast, but it was only spitting snow. The top of the pickup was just a dot peeking over the snowbank behind us and the trees started to swallow us up, and it seemed more and more like we were going where we ought to be. When we were about a mile and a half from the cabin, the snow started coming down heavier; but there wasn't much wind, and we were dressed for it. The only sound was the skis cutting through the powder and the poles punching in beside them, and the snowflakes hitting the snow, which you can't really hear, but it seems like you can.

We came to the one long slope between the road and the cabin. A soft wind had come up, and we stopped to look over the shallow valley and listen. It sounded like a long sigh that never runs out. When I was six, just before he died, my granddad told me that if the spirits of the Bannock and Shoshone and Northern Paiute did hang out in these hills, that wind was how they got around.

Becky looked down the slope. "That's a little steep for me," she said. "How do you slow down?"

"Two ways," I said. "You can snowplow"—and I fixed my skis, toes in—to show her—"or you can fall down. Actually there are three ways. You slow down when you get to the bottom."

"Pretty glib for a fella that's about to leave his virginity in the woods," she said, and took off. She fell three times.

"You learn quick," I yelled when she got down. I didn't

| 113

fall at all, until I got to the bottom and she pushed me over.

When we got to the cabin, snow was piled up about three-quarters of the way up the door, so the first thing we did was go through the window of the shed for the shovel. It took ten or fifteen minutes of hard work to get the place open, with Becky cheering me all the way. Then I shoveled out the door to the shed because that's where the wood was. I brought some in while Becky took the protective covering off the furniture and the bed, and I panicked and went back outside and shoveled a path from the cabin to the shed. I probably would have shoveled a path back out to the road if she hadn't stopped me.

Becky stuck her head out the door. "Come in here, we'll have some lunch."

That sounded safe enough. "Be in in just a sec," I said, and leaned the shovel up against the shed. Boy, this was scary stuff. The closest I'd come to having sex before was when I was a sophomore and reached inside this girl's blouse after a dance up at the school. I won't tell you her name; but it got going too fast, and I ended up getting scared and jumping out of her car. She called me some pretty bad names. With that kind of blotchy record, I had to be a little tentative.

Becky had a fire in the woodstove and one in the fireplace when I came in. She was warming up some bean and bacon soup on the stove and making sandwiches on the breadboard. When I got my coat off, she came over and gave me a long wet kiss and then just stood there looking at me, smiling.

114

"We probably should eat first," I said, looking over at the half-made sandwiches and the soup starting to boil on the stove.

She nodded. "Probably we should," she said. "Woman does not live on love alone." She smiled and looked at me again for a second. "Are you nervous?"

"No, why?"

She shrugged. "I guess I am. A little."

"Okay, well, yeah. I guess a little. A lot."

She put her hand on my cheek. "We can go as slow as we want. It'll work out just fine. If it doesn't we'll try again."

"Ah." I nodded. "The trial-and-error method. I've heard of it."

"Yeah, well," she said, "let's try to go light on the errors."

We ate and talked about other things, like where the basketball team would play their games and school and plans after graduation. Becky was set up to go to a small college down south of San Francisco. She'd already been accepted. I hadn't even applied anywhere yet. All I knew was I was getting out of Trout. What I really wanted to do was find out if there was a Podunk college anywhere south of San Francisco that would take an out-of-stater with a 2.46 grade point average, but I was being cool about that. I didn't want Becky to think I'd be following her all over the country. That is, unless she wanted me to.

My war with Jasper and Lednecky seemed over. Both of them were plenty willing to let it die, and I was all for that. Neither of them spoke to me unless they had to, and I gave them no trouble. My fears that Lednecky would flunk me in U.S. government turned out to be just fears. He didn't want me back. I was getting my C.

And Washington was tearing up the league in basketball. We'd already played them once, and he was awesome. They used a man-to-man defense, and he stalked Boomer all over the court. He blocked four of Boomer's shots and just stood there after each one, waiting for Boomer to blow. He's smaller than Boomer, but built like crazy, and Boomer wasn't about to get into it. At least not from the front. Boomer's not afraid of getting hurt, but he's terrified of getting humiliated. He averages about fourteen points a game, and Washington held him to three. I had to get a good hold on myself to keep from jumping up and screaming every time he put a move on Boomer or knocked the ball back in his face. At halftime down in the locker room, when Boomer was abusing him in the safety of those four walls, Carter told him to show Washington up on the court or shut his damn mouth. Boomer had a *bad* second half.

It was starting to seem there really was justice in the world. I hadn't got all the things I thought I wanted, like being a football star and all; but Washington was getting even with Boomer in ways I could never hope to, Jasper's and Lednecky's stuff seemed less and less important all the time, and I was out at Becky Sanders's cabin, getting ready to make love with Becky Sanders. Priorities, as Dakota would say.

Anyway, we covered all that ground over soup and sandwiches. The fire in the fireplace was burning down, and Becky went over to put more wood on it. She sat down on the bed, which was one of those that comes out of a couch, and motioned me over. All the talk had loosened me up, and I thought I had things under control; but my heart shot straight up into my throat. The plain ugly truth of the matter was I just wasn't ready. Think Boomer Cowans could have a field day with that?

It's a strange thing about life: how it keeps throwing you that inside curve to keep you off-balance, keeps setting you up for one thing, then showing you another.

Becky took off my shirt and had me lie down on the bed; then ran her fingernails lightly in circles, slowly over my back and up into my hair. She massaged my shoulders and kissed the nape of my neck. When she took off her blouse and we crawled under the covers, I said, "Becky, I don't think I can do this."

She smiled and kissed me on the forehead and said something I hope I'll always remember about sex. She said, "It's a funny thing about things like sex, that we're supposedly not supposed to do. Once it's okay to do it, it's okay not to." She kissed me again and whispered, "It's okay not to."

We were quiet for a little while, and I finally said, "Do you think there's something wrong with me?"

She laughed. "There are probably lots of things wrong with you, but what you're thinking isn't one of them. Sex is scary business, and it's probably best to wait until you're really ready. I've done it because I thought I was supposed

| 117

to, and I've done it because I really wanted to, and let me tell you, supposed to doesn't cut it."

I wanted to ask her if she'd done it a lot, but it didn't seem like I should. I knew she'd had a pretty heavy relationship with a college kid when she was off at one of those summer workshops, but we'd never talked much about him. All she said was that that was other times and other places. And she lived on the East Coast all her life before her sophomore year, close to Washington, D.C., and they say you grow up a lot faster there. Anyway, I didn't want to pry.

I didn't have to. Madame Sanders was also a mind reader. She said, "Not a whole lot of times, Louie. Don't worry about it. Right now, it's just you and me."

I was pretty sure her past didn't really bother me, though I'd get a little twinge sometimes. Actually I was glad to be with someone who knew enough about all this craziness to let me off the hook.

"You disappointed?" I asked.

She laughed and kissed me again. "You know what the very best thing about making love is?" she said. "It's before and after. It's lying together, taking care of each other and getting as close as we can. You don't really have to have sex to make love."

So Becky and I made love without having sex, and when I look back on it now, when everything's irreversible, I wouldn't have it any other way.

It's funny. You think you really know a girl. You spend as many of your waking hours as you can being with her and talking and asking questions, and you think you know it all. Then you spend a weekend like we did, and you find you didn't know your rear end. You get *so* close. Your conversations take on new meanings. I mean, there are ways of showing your weaknesses—your vulnerability—that aren't scary when you're that close, when most of your communication with each other is through touch. What an amazing roller coaster we're on.

We lay there in the early-morning hours with the fire burning down to embers, just kind of wrapped around each other, coming in and out of sleep, and I said, "Becky, I'm scared about you going to California."

She said, "Yeah, me, too."

"I mean, I'm scared for me," I said. "When you go down there, you're gone. I'm scared to lose this—you."

"Me, too."

We lay there awhile longer, and I said, "Is it crazy to want to be happy?"

"I don't know," she said. "It's probably crazy to think you're going to be all the time."

"I just want it to stay like this," I said. "What's wrong with that?"

She snuggled in under my arm. "The only reason it's like this now is that it *isn't* like this all the time," she said. "My shrink used to say, 'How can you know good if you don't know what bad is?'"

"God," I said, "I hate it."

She kissed me and said, "I love it."

After a while she said, "My going to California doesn't mean things won't work out with us or that they will. But there's a big challenge for me there. It's big and scary and anonymous. And it isn't my territory. I'm going down there like I own the place and see what happens. Who knows? I might be back by Halloween."

I forced it out of my mind because she started kissing and rubbing me again, and just before I finally drifted off, I remember being amazed at how much farther off Jasper and Lednecky and Boomer seemed. All my wars back in Trout didn't amount to a medium-sized compost heap. For a little while I was free of all that. If Becky had stayed around, I think I could have stayed free.

# CHAPTER 12

I SAID EARLIER how I think relationships work. I still wonder sometimes if ours was good enough to stand what would have happened in the next few years. It sure seemed like it was, but I'm no dummy—despite my 2.46 grade point average—I know things can change. Becky said if we *should* be together, we would, that things have a way of working themselves out. I wasn't that confident. Things seem to have a way of screwing up pretty bad before they get around to working themselves out. I just didn't want it to be one of those deals where we went off in different directions and never saw each other again except to say hi and be uneasy at Christmas parties.

That was all pretty scary, but it didn't seem to get in the way of all the fun and quiet good times we had together. Becky had a nice way of reassuring me and making me believe that whatever was going on at the time was all that needed our attention. Anyway, that's all rhetorical now, as they say, because Becky's not alive anymore. I mean, she's dead. Things didn't work out.

It was Saturday, March 21. Basketball season was over, and spring was right on time. The dirty snowbank piled up the length of Main Street was melting so fast in the fifty-five-degree breeze you could almost see it dropping. Jelly rolls were popping up all over the place. The sky was blue and clear, and I was out on the island, hosing six months of sediment out into the street. It was the first weekend of the year I worked without a coat.

Carter was there, leaning against the oil cabinet, talking about how he wished our school had baseball instead of track because track is such a pain in the butt. The reason we don't is that the diamond is usually covered with snow until late in the season. The track is, too, but we run on the back roads until it melts down. Our high jumper actually practices his form over a snowbank in a rubber suit.

I was washing down the pumps when Dakota streaked by in Doc Hamilton's makeshift ambulance, siren screaming, horn blasting. Carter said he must be going down to Cougar Mountain Lodge to get a sandwich. It was about one in the afternoon.

"Wanna go bowling tonight?" Carter asked. "What time do you close?"

"Nine," I said, "but I've got a date." We don't keep the place open till midnight until trout season opens in early June.

Carter shook his head. "Whipped," he said. "Never seen anybody so whipped." He laughed. "Can't blame you, though. Maybe I'll get a date with Sandy. Wanna go bowling if I can drum up a date?"

It sounded fun. "Sure," I said.

"Okay if I use your phone?"

"Just leave a dime on Norm's desk."

"Charge it," he said, and disappeared into Norm's office.

Brenda drove in the south entrance and pulled up beside the pumps.

"Hi," I said. "Need gas?"

She shook her head. Her face was chalky white. "Louie," she said, "I have some horrible news." She swallowed.

Norm, I thought. Something happened. The ambulance.

"Becky's been in an accident. Just over the hill at the bridge. She swerved to miss some kids on a motorcycle and hit the side of the bridge. The car went into the river." Brenda lowered her eyes.

"She can swim," I said. "The water's shallow there—"

"She's dead, Louie. She hit the windshield when the car hit the bridge."

"She always wears seat belts," I said. "She *always* wears her seat belt."

Brenda just shook her head. "The ambulance is there now. Dakota couldn't do a thing. Oh, Louie, I'm so sorry."

I flashed for a second on Becky darting out from beneath the covers to throw a log on the fire, her muscular legs flexing as she scooted to the fireplace. Alive.

Then my chest and throat clogged in panic. "Tell Carter to watch the place!" I said. "Please! Get somebody to watch the place!" I sprinted to the pickup, thinking somehow I could still save her. Brenda let me go.

When I got to the bridge, the wrecker was just pulling up. Dakota was slamming the back door of the ambulance. I stopped and got out slowly, staring straight at him. He grimaced and shook his head. I walked over and looked in the back window, at the long lump that was Becky just a few minutes ago.

"Dakota, can't you do something?" I asked. My voice sounded a long ways off.

He shook his head again. "I'm sorry, Louie. I know that doesn't mean a damn thing, but I'm sorry as hell."

I backed away from the ambulance and looked over the edge of the bridge at her car. The front was stuck in the riverbed, but the back of the roof and the tail were well above water. It couldn't have been more than four feet deep there. I started down through the brush.

"Don't go down there, Louie!" Dakota hollered.

I stopped and looked up at him, then continued down.

"Damn it, Louie!" he screamed. "Get back up here!" He closed his eyes. "Her blood is all over."

I stopped and sat down and stared at the car.

"Come on back up, son," he said again. "Come up and go home. There's nothin' you can do. Give yourself a break."

Dakota's been driving the ambulance almost as long as

124

he's been running the chain at football games. I guess he's seen a lot of that kind of thing. In a town this size, if somebody gets it, it's always somebody you know. Just last year he had to pull Zack Cameron out of his logging truck after the brakes locked and the whole load shifted forward, severing off the top of the cab and the top of Zack right with it. Dakota had to tell Zack's wife. He knew he couldn't help me, but he did get me to come up.

Just then Carter pulled up behind the pickup in his mom's car. He jumped out but stopped when he saw my face.

"Somebody watching the station?" was all I could think of.

He nodded. "Brenda's there."

I looked over at the ambulance and back at him and shrugged. Tears welled up in his eyes. I know he wanted to help me somehow, hug me, something, but his feet were glued to the spot. "I'll follow you back," he said.

I nodded.

It's funny. You get around a girl for a while, somebody you love and care about and respect, and you start doing things she'd approve of. You get to asking yourself how what you're doing would look to her, even if she's not around at the time. I didn't know where to go—couldn't think what Becky would want me to do—so I just drove slowly on through town. People stared at me from the sidewalk and through store windows; I could feel it. News travels fast. As I passed the turnoff to Carter's place, I waved him off, then headed for the lake, across the spillway and into the woods, out to the meadow where we used to park. I hiked across it and up into the woods, coming out at the shoreline about three miles north of the city dock, and walked another three or four miles along the shore. The funny thing about that afternoon is I can't remember anything I thought. Pretty soon it was dark, and five or six hours of my life were gone nowhere.

There was a pretty good moon—maybe just less than half—and I didn't have any trouble working my way back down the shoreline and over the hill to the meadow. The big pine cast a long, dim shadow clear back to the pickup. I walked over and sat down under it.

I've never been really religious, at least not in the way most people think of it. I mean, I light the candles sometimes at the Episcopal church; but that's mostly because they need somebody to do it, and it's easier than saying no when Reverend Watts calls and asks. But I pray sometimes, when I think it's God's business. I don't ask Him to give me things or make me better than somebody, but when something comes up that nobody can help me with and that I just can't understand by myself, I'll pray. Up until that day I felt like I had a pretty good relationship with Him.

So I gave it a go, sitting there under the tree. I looked through the branches and past the moon and right up at heaven and I said God, I don't get this, and it just isn't acceptable. I didn't do anything to deserve it. Nothin'. If there's a good reason, then you owe me an explanation, so let's have it. And I don't want to hear that you work in strange and wondrous ways that we don't understand be-

126

cause I've heard that before—every time something happens that's so ugly nobody can believe it. You just figure out a way to give me an answer, or you can count me out.

God didn't say diddly. The branches moved a little in the breeze, and the moon just kept shinin' on.

I said that's not good enough, and waited a little while longer.

Nothin'.

I said after what all had gone on that day, it wouldn't be totally out of place to give me some kind of answer, damn it.

Same response.

Sometimes when things are really going bad and everything around you has turned brown and you feel like a part of it all, instead of trying to make things better, you try to make them worse. I don't know why that is, but it is. After I figured I'd given Lord God Almighty plenty of time to answer and He didn't, I walked over to the pickup and dragged my granddad's old double-bitted ax out of the bed and came back and brought that tree to the ground. I'm sorry I did it now. It was big and tall and stood there like a king, and it was one of the nicest memories I had of Becky's and my first time together. But I dropped it. It must have taken me forty-five minutes, but I just stood there blasting away and screaming, "Is this yours? How do you like it? Is this yours? How do you like it?"

Then I drove back.

# CHAPTER 13

WHEN I PULLED UP to the house, Brenda's face was staring at me out through the kitchen window. I imagine she'd probably been there for a long time, hoping I'd come home before doing anything foolish. As I came through the kitchen door, she turned to face me, registering some shock at my appearance. "Are you all right?" she asked quietly.

I nodded and said yeah, that I'd been trying to work things out. She came over and hugged me. I could feel her tears against my neck, but by the time I pushed her away, gently, her eyes were dry and clear. Brenda's tough. Tough as hell. Three years ago, when my uncle got cancer and died miserably, by inches, she kept my aunt occupied at least six hours a day for more than seven months and still got all her other work done. The only time she broke was when she thought she was alone. She still doesn't know I saw her pounding her pillow and cussing God for not getting it over with. I guess our family has given the Old Geezer a rough go over the last few years.

"I know you don't feel like eating," she said, "but it would be good if you did. Norm's already eaten, but there's food in the oven."

I nodded. "Where is he?"

"Out looking for you," she said. "He should be back soon." It was a little after ten. Tracy was in bed.

The kitchen door opened, and Norm came through. He stopped, and we looked at each other for a second. My eyes dropped, and he walked over to put a hand on my shoulder. In Trout that's as close as a man gets to hugging another man.

"Bad break," he said.

I nodded.

He took a deep breath. "Well, this can't get us anywhere. Have something to eat, and we'll play it by ear."

Somehow we got through the rest of the evening, talking and watching TV. Norm and Brenda filled in all the silent moments they could, keeping me at least partially preoccupied.

When the late movie was over and they were playing "The Star-Spangled Banner," I figured we'd all had enough. "Look," I said, "I'm going for a short drive. Just for a little while."

Brenda shot a quick uneasy glance at Norm.

"I'm okay," I said. "I just want to be alone for a little while. I'm not going to do anything stupid." I smiled at her. "Really, Brenda, it's okay."

I drove down the deserted main street. The Buckhorn had closed a few minutes ago, and the people going home were the only action anywhere. I took a left at the Mercantile and a right at the next block and found myself in front of Becky's place. A light burned in the living room, and smoke poured out of the chimney. Mr. Sanders was alone in there, probably being eaten up. I had to go in.

He opened the door and invited me in. "Sit down," he said. "How're you doing?"

"Okay, I guess. How about you?"

He shrugged and nodded.

I glanced around the room. Becky was everywhere, her piano in the corner, a reproduction of "Starry Night" on the wall above the couch, an open box of medals she'd won for music and debate and all kinds of awards for scholastic stuff lying on the couch.

I sat on a three-legged stool next to the fireplace. Mr. Sanders sat back down on the couch and laid the box of awards in his lap. He absentmindedly picked up one of the medals, fingered it for a minute, and looked up at me. "It's a bitch, isn't it?"

"Yeah," I said. "A bitch."

"Louie," he said, "you're the first person I thought of. I've been around long enough to see death—stupid, senseless death—but I don't think I could have handled it at your age. Not with someone I loved."

130

"I got no choice."

"Yeah. Listen, how about a beer? I know it's probably not the best thing for a lawyer to get hauled up for 'contributing,' but under the circumstances I think it might be overlooked." He didn't wait for an answer, just went into the kitchen. I heard the caps pop, and in a second he was handing me one.

He sat back down. "She told me about your trip to the cabin."

My head snapped up. "She said—"

"Yeah, I know. She didn't want you to be uneasy around me. She wanted us to be friends, you and me."

I said I thought I'd like that.

"Is it okay?" I said.

"What?"

"Becky and me. At the cabin."

He smiled and closed his eyes, and a tear started down his cheek. "Yeah," he said, "it's okay." He took a swallow of beer and said, "Becky and I, we were friends. You don't see many kids and parents getting along the way we did. I trusted her; she could do pretty much what she wanted. We gave each other a lot of room, especially since the divorce, but we hung onto each other to beat hell."

All of a sudden he stood up and flung his bottle, exploding it against the fireplace. "Why?" he yelled. "Why? What the hell is she doing dead?"

I walked up behind him and put my hands on his shoulders.

"I'm sorry, Louie," he said. "I'll get it under control."

"It's okay." I kind of laughed. "Christ, I chopped down a

hundred-and-fifty-foot tree tonight, and it still wasn't enough."

He looked past me. "Her mom's flying in tomorrow," he said. "I can't tell you how I'm not ready for that."

"Bad news, huh?"

He smiled. "Bad news would be good news compared to this. She'll come sweeping in here and take over, and the funeral will turn into a circus, and I'm just not strong enough to stop her right now." He looked at me. "Listen, go home and try to get some sleep. You're going to need it."

I nodded and headed for the door. As I turned the knob, Mr. Sanders said, "Louie."

"Yeah?"

"Mr. Rodrick from Forest Lawn called this afternoon. He wanted to know where she parted her hair." His head dropped. "I couldn't remember."

I saw her long brown hair flowing over her shoulders and down around her breasts. She was laughing. "In the middle," I said.

# CHAPTER 14

MONDAY, the day of the funeral, was clear and even warm for that time of year. I wanted the weather to be crappy; but the *Farmer's Almanac* said there would be high pressure with a warming trend, and by God, there was high pressure with a warming trend.

Becky's mom had called on Sunday afternoon to ask if I'd consider being a pallbearer. I said no way. I was polite and everything, but I couldn't see any way in the world I'd be able to be there when they put her in the ground. In fact, I hadn't made up my mind whether to go to the service at all.

They had it at the Red Brick Church because it's the biggest one in town, and even though Becky had been baptized in the Episcopal Church, her mom wanted to accommodate the largest number of people possible. And she brought her own preacher along, all the way from the East Coast. Mr. Sanders told me later that was because she didn't want some hick town Bible thumper presiding over the most important event of their lives. She was every bit the rip Becky said she was.

School got out at eleven-thirty, so everyone could go home and eat and get dressed in time for the one o'clock service. All the stores in town advertised they would be closed from noon until four "In Memoriam." Becky was getting as much consideration as a football game.

I skipped school Monday morning—I don't think anybody really expected me to be there—and drove out to the bridge. For some reason I felt the need to torture myself. Norm says people do that. I kicked around the sand beside the river where she'd gone in and thought of a million ways she could still be alive. The kids on the motorcycle— it was a Honda 90—had been using the broken white line as a slalom course and apparently didn't even see what happened until Becky was already past them and in the river. They got scared and took off; but there were witnesses, and they were caught even before they could get home. The driver, Craig Martens, is only thirteen. He didn't even have a license. Don't think I didn't consider finding him and beating him beyond recognition, because I did consider it, but I figured nothing I could do would make him hurt any worse than he already did. If she'd met

134

that stupid motorcycle *anywhere* but where she did, she could've just gone in the ditch.

Anyway, I decided I could hold my own memorial services there at the river and bypass Mrs. Sanders's show at the church, so I stayed and skipped flat rocks across the water and talked to myself and to Becky and cried a little bit. I even tried to make a deal with God there for a second, but that cheapened everything, so I got off it.

By one or so I thought I had everything pretty much taken care of, so I drove back to town. The place looked deserted—the street empty, all the doors locked—and suddenly I felt the urge to say good-bye formally, like everyone else. I was dressed a little shabby—T-shirt, Levi's, and sneakers—but I remembered Reverend Watts told me once the Lord didn't care how I looked when I came to His house, so I figured they'd probably let me in.

It was about one-thirty when I got there, and the service had already started. A large crowd was gathered on the lawn by the entrance, and at first I thought I'd missed it; but there were just so many people the church wouldn't hold them. There was a loudspeaker rigged up above the door so the people outside could hear. I couldn't find a place to park, so I left the pickup in the middle of the road on the next block and walked back.

The big-city preacher's voice boomed the Lord's Prayer through the speakers as I walked toward the church. I'll bet Lednecky would give something very close to his manhood to have that guy's set of pipes. As I approached, the crowd sort of parted to let me through. I guess they knew I was one of the A number one grievers. I worked my way

| 135

through the crowd in the outer foyer and finally into the main congregation room. Up front Becky's casket lay wide open. Off to the left, in a special section that was shrouded behind a misty white veil, were Mr. and Mrs. Sanders and some aunts and uncles. Mr. Sanders had saved me a seat beside him, and when he saw me, he motioned me over; but I shook my head and stood leaning against the back wall as the congregation sang five verses of "The Old Rugged Cross." Then the big-city preacher stepped up again and let us have it. He talked about the light that had been taken from our midst, the song that died before it could be sung, the play that closed after such a brief but glorious run, and a couple more like that that I don't remember. Then he recounted her accomplishments one by one. The place was breaking up. He had the whole town in the palm of his hand, and *he didn't even know her!*

I started to work my way back out and had made it to the door leading back to the outer foyer when I heard him say, "Why, oh Lord? Why, in the prime of her young life was she stricken down?"

He paused. I was glued to the spot and could feel bad times moving in quick.

"We cannot answer these questions alone. But we know that you sometimes move in strange and mysterious ways that we, lost in our earthly ignorance, cannot understand."

He shouldn't have used the "strange and mysterious ways" defense. I could have held it together if he hadn't said that. All of a sudden I heard myself yelling, "Why are you saying that? He doesn't move in strange and mysterious ways. He doesn't move at all! He sits up there on His fat butt and lets guys like you earn a living making excuses for all the rotten things that happen. Or maybe He does something low-down every once in a while so He can get a bunch of us together, scared and on our knees. Hell with Him!"

I started to move out but figured as long as I'd gone this far . . . "And why are you trying to make us cry? We'll cry; we're gonna cry anyway. But Becky didn't care about all that crap. She liked to laugh and cry and eat burgers and make love and be with people she liked. Talk about that! Why don't you talk about that?"

I was just getting warmed up, but I felt hands clamp down on both my arms. Carter and Boomer rushed me through the crowd.

"Go easy, Louie, go easy," Carter was saying over and over.

Boomer kept saying, "It's okay, man. It's okay, man." To tell you the truth, the reason I went so willingly was hearing the kindness in Boomer's voice. I don't know where it came from, and I don't imagine it stayed long; but it was the real thing.

When we got outside, I relaxed for a second, then broke free and sprinted for the pickup. I think Boomer tried to stop me; but Carter must have caught him, and they let me go. I was across the spillway, onto the old road, and parked out at the meadow before I even thought about what I'd done. Then I thought about Norm and Brenda and how they must have been shocked and embarrassed, and for their sakes I was sorry; but I didn't feel sorry for doing it. I was still way too angry and hurt.

Boy, it's a tribute to the people of Trout that they didn't organize a vigilante committee and string me up.

I stayed out there until after nine and decided to go on home. As I drove down Main Street, I noticed the "Closed" sign was still up in the window at the Buckhorn, so I went around back to let myself in, hoping maybe I'd run into Dakota. Donkey Caulder was propped up against the outer back wall with his bottle in a paper sack, but he wasn't drinking it. He looked asleep. I shook his arm and said, "Hey, man, if you're cold, I'm going to be in here awhile. Come on in."

He mumbled something that ended with "bullshit" and dropped his head to his knees.

"Well," I said, "it's open," and went on in.

The place hadn't been open all day, so it was clean. The lights were out, but Dakota had forgotten to turn off the beer signs, so there was an eerie dim light across the room. I sat down in a corner over by the pool table and stared at the illusion of water tumbling over the falls on the Oly sign. There was a horseshoe with a little sign over it that said "Good Luck."

Good luck.

Dakota came in the side door. "Figured that must be you," he said. "Want some company?"

I nodded. "Yeah, I guess I do."

He stood there in the doorway and just looked at me. Finally he said, "Louie, it ain't safe."

"What's that?"

"Trout. School. Football. This here bullshit life. It ain't safe. None of it."

"You're right," I said. "It's a lot of things, but safe ain't one of them. I gotta tell you, Dakota, I don't get it. Man, what did Becky ever do to get killed? What did any of us ever do? It just isn't right."

"Nope," he said. "It ain't right, that's for sure."

I just shook my head, and for only the second time the tears came. And man, they came. I must have lost five pounds. Dakota stood there and watched me. "It's just not fair," I said. "What kind of worthless God would let this happen?"

"Louie," he said, "I ain't an educated guy; but I listen pretty good and I see pretty good, and one thing I'm pretty sure of is that if there's a God, that ain't His job. He ain't up there to load the dice one way or the other."

I didn't say anything; I didn't get it.

Dakota said, "Boy, if you come through this, you'll be a man. There's one thing that separates a man from a boy, the way I see it, and it ain't age. It's seein' how life works, so you don't get surprised all the time and kicked in the butt. It's knowin' the rules."

"The rules," I said. "How can you know the damn rules? They keep changing."

"Naw, they don't," he said. "It's just that you have to learn the new ones as you go. That's the hard part. Learnin' the new rules when they show theirselves. You go on blamin' God, you get no place. You got to pay attention to how things work. Ya got to understand that the reason some things happen is just because they happen. That ain't a good reason, but that's it. You put enough cars and trucks and motorcycles on the road, and some of 'em gonna run into each other. Not certain ones neither. Just

| 139

whichever ones do. This life ain't partial, boy."

"I don't know," I said, after thinking about it a minute. "I need the rules to be a lot simpler. Easier. I can't take it like this."

Dakota walked over around behind the bar and opened a cabinet and took out an old checkerboard and some chips. "Come 'ere a minute," he said. "I wanna show you somethin'."

I went over and sat on a stool. "I'm not sure I'm up for checkers," I said.

"Indulge an old fart," he said. "This ain't regular checkers. You might learn somethin'. Now here's how it works. You can jump as many places as you want, backwards or forwards. Don't need a king. You go first."

I didn't quite get it, but I moved a man across several squares and took one of his chips.

"That it?" he said.

I nodded.

Then he jumped all my men in one move and took them off the board. "I win. Wanna play again?"

"Sure," I said, "if I can go first again."

"You can go first again." He set them up, and I took all his chips in a move.

"Damn," he said. "That puts us even. Wanna go another one?"

"I go first?"

"You go first." He set them up again, and I took them all in one move again.

"That's only two out of three," he said. "One more?"

I looked at him setting them up like it meant something,

and said, "Hey, Dakota, you know this isn't a lot of fun."

"Ain't, is it?" he said. "Not hardly worth playin'. Funny, too, 'cause the rules are simple and easy."

My Felix the Cat light bulb popped on. I nodded. "Yeah."

We sat and played some real checkers for a while, and I got beat a lot. I'd win once in a while, but not often. Then we played some pool. I never won at that, but I had a few moments. Finally, when the sun was starting to come up, Dakota told me I better be getting home before my momma woke up and crapped her drawers with worry. I tried to thank him for getting me through the night, but he just waved me off.

As I started out the door, he stopped me. "Louie."

"Yeah?"

"If you was walkin' in the middle of the road an' you saw a big ol' truck comin' right at ya, you wouldn't stop an' ask the Lord to get you out of the way, would ya?"

"No," I said. "I'd probably just get off the road."

"Well then, don't be goin' askin' Him to get ya out of the way of all the other crap that's comin' at ya." He held up his hook and looked at it. "You go on an' take care of it yourself."

# CHAPTER 15

THE FIRST THING I did in the way of making amends for my outburst at the funeral was stop by the parsonage on my way home to apologize to Reverend Miller for opening my big mouth in his church, even though he wasn't the one preaching. I told him I was particularly sorry for saying "guys like you" and hoped he didn't think I included him in on that. I hate it when someone calls me "guys like you." It usually casts you with a lot that can be identified by one ugly, distasteful characteristic. I didn't apologize for my point of view, though, just didn't mention it. Reverend Miller assured me that he understood I was emotionally upset and that they were able to get the whole affair under control with little difficulty after I left. He said a few people were still upset and that I could probably expect them to act that way, but time would probably work it all out. Then he said maybe I could redeem myself by mowing the church lawn all summer. It would be a nice gesture to the church, and people could see that I was genuinely sorry.

I said I'd see.

Then I drove over to Mr. Sanders's house, hoping I hadn't lost it all with him. That scared me a lot. He met me at the door with a half smile, shaking his head. "Boy, you did it this time," he said. "I've had a dozen phone calls from people telling me how disgusted they are with you. Better come in before someone sees you and stirs up a lynch mob."

"Thanks," I said, and went on in. "Listen, I'm really sorry. I wasn't thinking of anyone but myself. No excuses, but I'm sorry."

He flipped his hand. "Don't apologize to me," he said. "I was probably as disgusted as you were." He laughed. "It's a good thing you didn't come here last night, though. Becky's mother would have clawed your eyes out and spit in the sockets."

I flinched.

"How about some breakfast?"

"I should be getting home. I haven't been home all night, and Norm and Brenda are probably worried. I've got to start getting things back together somehow."

"Yeah," he said. "Me, too. Listen, I'll give them a call and tell them I'll feed you and you'll be home in a little while."

I couldn't resist him, so I said go ahead. He called and then started some eggs and bacon. It occurred to me I hadn't eaten since Sunday night and was starved. Fred— he told me to call him that—ended up cooking me another full breakfast before I left. We talked a little about what should happen next but didn't really come up with much, other than to just wait and see how things went. He assured me that he would continue to defend my maniacal actions to anyone who brought them up. I told him to plead temporary insanity.

I left after we ate, and I went home, feeling a lot of responsibility for Norm and Brenda and how they must have felt. When I got in, Brenda was washing the breakfast dishes and Norm was reading the *Statesman*, getting ready to go to work. I told them I thought I'd pass on school one more day and see if I could sleep. After that, I promised, I'd get it back together and take care of business. Then I apologized to them for what I'd done.

Brenda dried her hands and came over and hugged me—for a long time. "Let's just let it ride," she said. "There's nothing we can do about it now but forget it."

That sounded good to me.

I was in the bathtub when Norm came into the bathroom to brush his teeth before going to work. He stood looking at me a second and just said, "It's been a rough weekend."

"Yeah. Seems like everything I touch lately turns dark brown."

He leaned against the sink and folded his arms. "What you did yesterday might not have been the smartest thing you could have done." Norm understates things well.

"I know," I said. "I'm really sorry—"

"You didn't hurt us," he said. "Only caused a little discomfort. But you said things that people probably didn't need to hear. You have to remember that even though she was your girl friend, Becky meant something to other people, too. And their perspectives are just as important to them as yours is to you."

I looked down at the water. "I don't know why I did it, Norm. Every funeral I've ever been to. they say the same stuff, and I just didn't want to see her go down the tube like Grandpa and Ronnie Dicks and Mrs. Lopez." Tears welled up in my eyes again. Becky was as dead as they were, no matter how loud I screamed in church. "I'm just really sorry for you guys. I know it's really hard to explain a kid who does stuff like that."

Norm smiled. "I don't know," he said. "I've never known anyone who *had* to explain a kid who does stuff like that. Besides, I'm not going to explain it. You're seventeen. You did it. You explain it."

I gave him the okay sign. "Right."

"Listen," he said, "I've got a contract to haul eight thousand gallons of gas and diesel into Stibnite, and I could use some help. If we use both trucks, we could get a load apiece per day for the next four days. They have to have it by the beginning of next week. What do you say?"

"Sure, but what about school?"

"I can get you out to work," he said. "I doubt there's anyone up there dying to see you. It probably wouldn't hurt if you stayed away for a few days. You should be able

| 145

to make up the work at home, shouldn't you?"

I nodded and stood up and asked him to hand me a towel. "Who's going to run the station?"

"Del Abbotts. He's been dying to get a little work somewhere since he retired from the mill. Says he's about to be the target of some serious spouse abuse if he doesn't get out of the house."

Boy, that Norm is always there. I can just see him figuring a way to get me out of school and away from Trout for a little while. I mean, they couldn't have needed all eight thousand gallons before the start of the week. What, were they going to use it faster than he could haul it in? He just figured a week away would soften things up a little. And the trip into Stibnite is a good one if you need time to think. It cuts about sixty-five miles on dirt roads into the backcountry following Elk Creek east for forty miles or so and then up the East Fork of the South Fork of the Salmon for another twenty-five. You can start at six in the morning and get home at six in the evening and not meet up with five other vehicles the whole time. All there is is water and mountains and animals and the sound of your truck.

That's what we did. I started every morning at six and he started at six-thirty, so he wouldn't have to eat my dust for twelve hours. Twelve hours alone every day for four days is a lot of time to think. That's what Norm wanted. I thought about Becky every minute of it, but I was getting a little distance. It became clear that I was going to have to go on and do whatever I was going to do.

Every day I stopped at a different spot for an hour to eat the sack lunch Brenda fixed me and stretch, and I noticed the woods a lot more than I did before I met Becky. There's a lot of life out there—big and little—and I saw it all, maybe cared about it a little more. I listened to the wind high up in the lodgepoles, watched the birds moving in from down south, and felt some sunlight. The third day I saw a herd of about eight or nine elk grazing in a meadow on the East Fork, where I'd stopped to eat. I watched for a long time before I tried to get a little closer and scared them away. I remember thinking I'll never be a hunter. You never know when you might gun down some young buck's girl friend.

It's amazing to me how fast time smooths things over. By Saturday evening, when we'd hauled the last load, I still missed Becky like crazy, and I've had plenty of hard times since; but the really vicious, almost unbearable edge was gone. I can't say how lucky I was to have Dakota and Norm and Mr. Sanders sticking by me—staying with me while I got crazy, pointing out ways to go—and Brenda for somehow making me know that no matter how bad it got, I wouldn't be alone.

Somehow I was sort of able to do what Becky said we should both do if we ever broke up: put it in a box and remember it as one of the nice things that happened.

I backslide from that every once in a while, when I just want to see her so bad I can't think of anything else, but seeing it gave me a place to start over.

# CHAPTER 16

I SHOWED UP to school a little late on Monday—not late enough to have to go for a tardy slip, but late enough so I wouldn't have to talk to anyone before class—and just slipped into my seat behind Carter. He waved to me without turning around and gave me thumbs-up. A few people looked over at me but went quickly back to their books. Mrs. Kjack was in the middle of *One Flew over the Cuckoo's Nest*, which, for the first time in my life, I'd finished ahead of her. I have a feeling the general public in Trout hasn't read it, or we wouldn't have. There are some books, like *Catcher in the Rye*, that have been banned in our school district, but the rule is a teacher is forbidden to use only those books that have been specifically banned. A book has to get some attention before it can get the ax, so Mrs. Kjack usually gets some mileage out of the good ones before they disappear. *Cuckoo's Nest* has been around awhile, but somehow it slipped by. Carter once told me we were going to read one about a professional baseball catcher who kept getting caught in bed with the team owner's wife, called *Catcher in the Raw*. Who knows?

Anyway, I opened my copy to the page she was talking about and slid down a ways in my seat, attempting to become part of the natural surroundings. A note landed in front of me. I looked up to see Carter's smiling mug. "Good to have you back," he whispered.

"Mr. Sampson, are you a part of this class?" Mrs. Kjack asked.

"Yes, ma'am," he said. "Just exercising a little of that civil disobedience you and that McMurphy guy have been talking about."

"Have you finished the book, Mr. Sampson?"

"Yes, ma'am."

"Then you've seen what happens to Mr. McMurphy."

"Yes, ma'am." He went back to his book.

I opened the note, visualizing Carter with a lobotomy. It said Coach Madison wanted to see me. I tapped Carter on the shoulder and whispered, "Why?" He shrugged without turning around, though he probably knew.

I tried to see Madison during my free period, but he had his algebra class then, so I took my sack lunch down to his room at noon. Unless you're hot for Spanish rice, Brenda makes a lot better lunch than they serve in the lunchroom.

"Hi, Coach," I said, sitting on his desk.

He looked up from some papers. "Oh, hi, Louie. Have a seat."

I smiled. "Already got one."

"That's not a seat. You're sitting on my geometry tests."

"Boomer Cowans sent me here to steal away with them," I said, getting up and moving to the chair beside his desk.

Madison smiled. "That's the best chance he's got to get a grade as high as a zero."

I said, "Carter said you wanted to see me."

He stared at me for a second. "Yeah. Having some hard times lately, huh?"

"Yeah, I guess so," I said. "It's working out, though."

He looked at my sandwiches. "I'll trade you a peanut butter and jelly for a salami." Madison's a bachelor.

"Sure." I handed over a sandwich.

He shook his head. "Boy, if it weren't for my superior bartering sense, I'd die of malnutrition." He doesn't look to be in danger to me. At about my height, he looks like Boomer stretched out. And is he ever studly-looking. That wavy blond hair and those light blue eyes have turned on more than one Cougarette.

"You keep trading with me," I said, "and you'll die of malnutrition anyway. When I fix my own, I have two Hostess fruit pies and a Coke."

He winced. "Listen, Louie, the reason I called you in here is to see if you're interested in turning out for track."

150

"I can't. I quit football. Jasper and Lednecky said I can't participate in any more sports."

"Is that in writing?"

"Nope," I said. "Not unless it's written down somewhere as a general rule."

"It's not," he said. "Coach Lednecky said it was, but I checked it out. No such thing."

"Well, it may not be in writing, but I doubt either of them will forget it was said."

He nodded and was quiet for a moment. "I think you could run," he said. "Why don't we give it a shot?"

"You know, Coach," I said, "you might not want to mess with those guys. They may not own this place, but you'd never know it from the way they act."

He nodded again and walked over to close the door. "Louie, let me tell you why I'm doing this, and this doesn't leave the room."

I said okay.

"I lost a girl friend once, when I was a sophomore at Black Hills. Her name was Sharon. We were rock climbing, and she fell. We should have been hooked up, but we weren't. She didn't even fall very far, but she landed on the back of her head and snapped her spinal cord. Instant." He snapped his fingers.

I started to say I was sorry but didn't get it out.

"If I hadn't had something physical to concentrate on, I'd have gone nuts," he said. "Absolutely nuts. Certifiable. You're going to need some of that now, and I've got the perfect thing. The two-mile."

"Two-mile?" I said. "You mean run a mile and then run one more?"

"That's generally how it's done. It would be perfect for you. No blinding speed, but a lot of guts. I saw that mile you ran at the first football practice."

"Two miles?" I said again. "Eight laps? Four and four? Six and two? Seven and one?"

"What do you think?"

"I hope Jasper and Lednecky fire you for asking," I said. "Really."

"Really, it sounds like something I could get into," I said. "My free time is killing me." It was true.

"I have to tell you there's one more reason," he said, "so you'll know where I'm at."

"Shoot."

"When Coach Lednecky put the contract out on Washington, I didn't say much. I knew it was cheap, and I knew Boomer would do it if he got the chance. When he did, I still didn't say much. I told you before, Louie, I care about sports. They're important to me. But I let Lednecky take all the pride out."

"Yeah," I said, "but what could you do? You're new. They'd have had you out of here before Thanksgiving."

"That's the excuse I used, but it just wasn't good enough. I'd rather not do it at all than do it like that."

I raised my eyebrows with nothing to say.

"I think everyone probably gets only a few chances in his life to make a stand for something he cares about, and I've blown one chance already. Now I don't want to do this just to go to war, so if you don't want to run, say so. But if you do, I'll go to the wall with it."

"Then let's do it," I said.

"Okay. Now remember, the goal is to get you running, not to take on the dragon. Got it?"

"Lead on, oh Lancelot," I said. "You know, Becky may have been right about you."

"How?"

"She said maybe you weren't just another dumb good-looking jock."

He stood up and punched my shoulder. "Look, we've got about twenty-five minutes left of lunch period. I asked if I could talk with them both at twelve-thirty. Let's go hit them with it together. They should be in Jasper's office now. We'll take 'em by surprise. If we pull it off, you can start running today."

Lednecky and Jasper were seated at Jasper's desk, finishing lunches sent up on trays by the school cooks. I remember thinking maybe they did own the place. It was pretty obvious they were surprised to see me with Madison.

"What's on your mind, Coach?" Lednecky asked, nodding in my direction.

Jasper just smiled.

We sat down. "I think I've got Louie talked into turning out for track," Madison said.

Lednecky sat forward and said, "Well you can just talk him out of it. You know the rule. What are you trying to do?"

"I'm trying to get Louie out for track. I *thought* I knew the rule, but when I went to check on it for sure, it didn't exist."

Lednecky's jaw tightened, but he didn't speak.

Jasper leaned back in his chair. "It's nothing we ever had to write down," he said. "In fact, it's been pretty much of a judgment call on the part of the principal and the athletic director in the past." Athletic director. That was a laugh. There's no athletic director here. I didn't laugh.

"Well then," Madison said, "I guess I need to question the judgment on this one. I need a distance man. Bad. When Louie ran the mile at the beginning of football season, the only guys to take him were Sampson and Cowans. You know what kind of chance I have of getting either of those guys to run the mile, much less the two." He paused and looked Jasper straight in the eye. "I think Louie can do the team some good."

Jasper looked at me. "Louie, could you step outside for a few minutes? I'd like to talk this over with Coach Lednecky and Coach Madison."

I stood up.

"Wait," Madison said. "This concerns him. I think he should be allowed to sit through it."

I raised my eyebrows to Jasper.

He shrugged. "Okay, sit down, Banks."

I sat.

Lednecky leaned forward again, and I got that feeling you get sometimes when you think you've been where you are before. "Let me get this clear in the beginning," he said. "Banks, you openly defied me on the football field last fall. As far as I'm concerned, you used up all your chances right there. You're not fit to be an athlete representing this school. And that's to say nothing of your desecration of young Miss Sanders's funeral—"

"Easy, Coach," Jasper said.

Lednecky sat back, his face beet red. The veins beside his eyes and in his neck bulged. Scary.

Madison spoke quietly, like he was trying to keep things from getting crazy. "My point is this. Louie showed up for football in top shape. He worked out harder than anyone on the team until the incident with the Washington kid. He doesn't drink or smoke that I know of, and he always met the curfew. I think he can cover a mile or two miles faster than anyone else I can get to run those distances. I don't care what he thinks of funerals or blacks or football or Trout High School or me, as long as he can produce. Now I'm the coach and I'm willing to work with him and I think he can produce."

Lednecky had regained most of his composure. "You seem to have missed the point, Coach," he said. "We're not just producing athletes here; we're building young men. Young men we can turn out into the community or send on to college and be proud of. Somewhere along the way we obviously failed in this case, and I don't want it to spread. One person with an attitude like Banks's can destroy a whole team." The Domino Theory of Rotten Apples.

Madison held his ground. "I have to disagree with you there, Coach," he said. "It might destroy your football team, but it won't bother my track team in the least. I'm not building young men; I'm building athletes. What they

| 155

do with that is their own business. Let the Marine Corps build young men. I'm giving these kids a chance to do something to the best of their ability, and that's all." He looked straight at Lednecky and said, "We can *show* them ways to live their lives, but we can't tell them."

Jasper folded his hands on his desk. "I have to agree with Coach Lednecky," he said coldly. Surprise of surprises. I have a feeling he was just itching to get Madison alone. "No athlete operates independently of his teammates. Not even in an individual sport like track. I think we'd be setting a poor precedent by letting Louie compete, and I think it would come back to haunt us." His eyes narrowed. "If you don't agree, maybe we should get someone to take over the track team."

Madison grimaced. I thought he was finished, but he'd come to get a job done. "Sir, we're talking about covering a certain amount of ground in a certain amount of time. Nothing more. Give us a shot, please."

Jasper shook his head. "I'm sorry, Coach. I've said all I have to say."

I looked at Madison and raised my eyebrows.

"That's the kind of smartass crap we won't tolerate, Banks!" Lednecky snapped.

"What?" I said in genuine surprise.

He pointed at me threateningly. "You know what I'm talking about!"

I looked back at my knees and made an effort to keep my smartass eyebrows still.

"Wait," Madison said. "How about this then? Louie won't work out with the team, and he'll travel to meets separately. The only time anyone on the team will even see him will be at meets. You can make sure everyone knows the story, so no one thinks he's getting away with anything. You can call it therapy or something. He won't have any influence on any of the team, except possibly to make them run faster."

Jasper was quiet for a second. Then he frowned and said, "Coach, you're walking on thin ice. I said that was all I had to say. Now why don't you two take off before you're late for fifth period?"

Madison shrugged and stood up.

I stood, nodded at both of them, and gratefully disappeared behind Madison.

"Boy," I said when we got out in the hall, "I don't think I could stand too many more swell things being said about me without getting the big head."

Madison just smiled and said to consider the source. "That's not the end of it," he said. Beads of sweat stood out on his forehead, and his shirt was soaked under the arms. "Those guys don't own this place. This is a public school paid for with public money."

I took a deep breath. "Man, you're looking to get your butt in a sling. Lednecky's already gonna be on you like stink on poop."

"It'll be worth it," he said as we walked into his room and closed the door, "if we can pull this off. Damn it, that makes me mad." He snapped his fingers. "Hey, your dad's on the school board. What do you think he'd think about this?"

I told him about how Norm wouldn't agree to bar me

from all extracurricular activities back when Jasper let me back in school.

"Well then, we have an ace," Madison said. "I won't use it unless we have to, and I have one trick I want to try before I do." He looked at his watch. "Bell's gonna ring. Get yourself to class. I'd hate to see what would happen if you had to show up in the office for a tardy slip now."

# CHAPTER 17

C OACH MADISON HAD one more trick all right. He really didn't want to go to the school board because he didn't want to put Norm on the spot. Norm wouldn't have cared; in fact, he'd probably have enjoyed it, but Madison didn't know him.

What he did was call Fred Sanders to see if there was a possibility that what Jasper and Lednecky were doing was illegal—like making some kid cut his hair or something. I couldn't believe it when he caught me between sixth and seventh periods to tell me what he'd done.

"You mean, take it to court?"

He nodded. "Sure, why not? A principal is allowed only so much power, just like anyone else. As near as I can tell, Jasper's taking way too much. And Lednecky shouldn't have any."

I was pretty willing to go along with anything. What could I lose? I suppose Lednecky could have flunked me in government, but that would look pretty fishy since I still had a strong C going in there. Besides, that would mean they'd have me back next year, and I had a feeling they were as tired of me as I was of them. "What did he say?" I asked.

"Said he'd look into it and get back to me," Madison said.

I just shook my head. I've never seen a teacher stand up to the principal before. Over anything. I was trying to imagine how Madison would look wandering the halls without a head.

"You have to draw the line somewhere," he said. "A man's position only allows him so much room. After he uses it all and grabs for more, it has to be brought to someone's attention. Jasper's like the rest of us. He has to face up to his responsibilities, too." His face was flushed. There was a lot more riding on all this than just me running.

The bell rang. "Go to class," he said. "I'll see you after school."

Kathy Collins came into my last-period journalism workshop with a note that said I was to report to the office when the bell rang. I immediately abandoned an article on the drill team's bake sale, so I could concentrate on worry-

160

ing. By the time the bell did ring I was sure those two bastards were going to tie me to Jasper's desk and beat the bottoms of my feet with hot spoons.

When I got there, Madison motioned me inside. Jasper and Lednecky looked like they hadn't moved since lunch. Jasper nodded. Madison stood in front of his desk.

"I had a phone call you two might be interested in," Jasper said. "From Fred Sanders."

I looked at the floor. Madison stared directly at Jasper.

"He said he had a long talk with you after Becky's funeral, Louie, and you two had ironed everything out."

"I guess so," I said, completely confused. "What does this have to do with me running track?"

"Nothing," he said, "except that he also said he thought you were aware of any mistakes you've made in the last year and felt it might do you a lot of good to get back into the mainstream of things. He asked if we could do anything along those lines."

Madison said, "Can you?"

"I see it this way," Jasper said. "If he can forgive Louie for that outburst at the funeral, we might at least be able to make a compromise." Boy, sometimes that man's logic amazes me. "Coach Lednecky and I have talked it over at length and have decided we'll let Louie run under the provisions you set down this noon. He doesn't practice with the team, and he has to get to meets some way other than on the team bus."

"He can ride with Floyd," Madison said. That's Floyd Fowler. He used to throw the discus and run the low hurdles, kind of a legend around Trout. Now he sort of acts as trainer at meets. He likes track, and it gives him a chance to get out of town once in a while. He has a hauling business, so he can pretty much call his hours.

"I don't care how you work it out," Jasper said, "but I'll hold you to it. Louie does this all on his own." He looked at me. "Is that agreeable with you, Banks?"

I nodded. "Yes, sir."

He pointed his finger at me and said in a low voice, "Mess this up once, and it's all over." Then he turned to Lednecky. "Anything to add, Coach?"

Lednecky shook his head. "Only that it's a lot farther than I'd have gone, but you already know that."

Jasper stood up. "Okay, that's it then." He paused. "You know, the thought crossed my mind that you two had something to do with this, with Fred calling. He swears you didn't, and I'm pretty sure you didn't have time. If I find out different—"

Madison raised his hands. "Would never have thought of it," he said. "Besides, I was in chem and basic math."

"Okay," Jasper said. "One other thing: There'll be an article in this week's school paper explaining why we're letting you turn out, Louie. We want it very clear that this is an exception to the rule. I thought you should know that before it happens. I like to treat people fair, let them know where they stand."

I nodded. "Okay, thanks." Boy, those guys were covering themselves every step of the way, but I wasn't about to argue. One thing I was starting to learn is that you zero in on what you need, and if you have to eat a little dark brown one to get it, open wide. You got to take care of yourself.

162

Out in the hall, Madison slapped me on the back. "We did it!" he whispered. "Damn it, we did it! Forget all that crap about the team and the newspaper. We went in there to get you running, and you're running." He put his arm across my shoulder. "Fred played it just right. I could kiss that guy! If we'd have done it my way, we'd have spent the rest of the season getting it solved. We're in the clear!" He punched me. "Head out to the gym. I'll be out in a minute to check you out some gear."

"Okay." I started down the stairs, feeling the best I'd felt since the weekend at the cabin.

Actually track season didn't start officially for another week, but the distance runners were already working out. You can't run two miles on talent alone, which I haven't got even if you could. You have to train. And train. And train. I didn't know it then, but I was up for anything.

I sat down in Madison's office, which is across the stage from Lednecky's, and waited. Within a few minutes he was there rummaging through the boxes of sweats. He decided to give me two sets, one medium and one extra-large. That way if we got more snow—or just cold—I could put one set over the other and go. He said we couldn't let anything slow me down, that we didn't have that much time.

All of a sudden a horrible thought struck me. "Coach," I said, "what if I can't do it? I mean, what if I'm not any good?" I felt like I owed him.

He was ahead of me. "Don't worry," he said. "I'm not expecting anything but for you to go out and run the best two-mile you want to. That's it."

"Sounds fair," I said, relieved, and continued digging

through the used jocks and socks. "I'm not used to that kind of coaching."

"I'm not used to coaching that way either," he said, "but here's the way I figure it. You got into shape for football by yourself. No coaching, just desire. If you have the same desire for this, I won't have to coach you at all, just sit around waiting for you to make me look good. I want you to forget about the Cougars and school records and points and all that and just concentrate on pushing yourself.

"Look," he said, pulling an old discolored magazine article from his clipboard. It was from a *Sports Illustrated* clear back in the middle sixties. "I was really young then, but this guy was my hero." There were pictures of a guy from Kenya, Africa, named Kip Keino, training for the 1500 meters, which was considered a distance then. "The writer asked him how far he ran every day, and he just smiled and shrugged. No idea. You know what he did? He just hauled across the countryside until he couldn't run anymore. That's when he figured he'd gone far enough. Trained alone." Madison turned the page. "And look at these other pictures. This maniac is smiling. He loves it!"

Sure enough, there was Keino striding over the crest of a long, steep hill with a great big grin on his face.

Madison slapped the article down on the taping table. "That's what athletics is all about. This guy was a world record holder." He boosted himself up onto the table. "I remember when Keino was at his peak; it was during the time when good Americans everywhere said that Negroes were great at sprints but they'd never take the whites in anything over a four-forty. Too lazy."

164

I said, "Someone ought to tell Henry Rono that."

"They probably did. That's why he's so fast."

"You going to run your whole track program that way?" I asked.

He shook his head. "You kidding? I'm going to run their butts off. Some of that desire is lacking in the general population. You got shoes?"

"Unh-unh," I said. "Not here. Got an old pair of high tops at home."

"What size?"

"Nine."

He dug through some boxes and tossed me one. "Don't say I never gave you anything."

"Adidas!" I said. I love Adidas.

"They're top of the line," he said. "Treat 'em good. They cost the taxpayers fifty bucks, and that's at a discount. Go ahead and get dressed. Since Lednecky and Jasper don't want you mixing with the team, you'll have to use this room and the coaches' shower, though I wouldn't recommend you shower while Lednecky's around."

I stripped and stuffed my clothes into Madison's locker.

"Here's the setup," he said. "I've laid out three courses for you to start with." He handed me three mimeographed maps. "The first two are about four miles apiece, and the third is seven, in case you want to keep track. You don't have to run those if you don't want to; you can run anywhere you'd like. But remember this: In this sport you get back *exactly* what you put in. If you're in good shape, you'll hit good times. If not, every race will be a miserable SOB."

Before I left, Madison said he didn't want me to run for time except in meets because he didn't want me creating psychological barriers for myself. Just run the way you feel, is what he told me; find the outer limit and push against it as long as I could. "Remember," he said, "you can always take one more step."

Boy, was I psyched. I spread analgesic on my chest and legs—it was about thirty-five or forty degrees out—and headed up toward the four-mile course that ran alongside the lake. On the way I stopped outside Mr. Sanders's office downtown. He was on the phone, so I just knocked on the window and pointed to the Cougar on my sweat shirt. He got a big grin on his face and gave me the okay sign. Then I headed on up.

About halfway through the course the first time I stopped and threw up. I hadn't done a lot of working out since football, except for cross-country skiing, and everything hurt. But throwing up doesn't mean a heck of a lot. Mostly it makes you feel better, so you can keep going and make yourself feel worse. I finished the course and ran it again. When I stopped, my head hammered with pain, and both sweat suits were soaked completely through. I jogged back to school, took salt, vitamin C, and about a half hour's worth of hot water.

The next couple of days were worse because it took the first mile and a half to work the soreness out, and I felt drained all the time. Madison said just to stay with it, and by Friday I began to get strength back and was even able to add a little mileage, proving I wasn't in as bad shape as I thought.

By the end of the second week I didn't run any of the mapped courses anymore. I'd just pick a direction and start running. Madison never asked how far I ran or got on me about anything. He just asked if I was satisfied with my workouts and gave me tips on how to relax my upper body when I ran and how to lengthen my stride.

Some days I'd go into the woods, where there was still lots of snow on the ground, and run through drifts and heavy brush and across meadows, never stopping for fear of freezing my legs. I wore old shoes on those days so I wouldn't wreck my Adidas. Other days I'd go down to the station and ride out into the valley with Norm, who was back to delivering stove oil and diesel in my absence, and run back.

One day I even went down to the bridge where Becky was killed. I started running upstream from where her car went in and ran all the way back to the spillway. Then I turned around and ran back to the bridge. When I finished, the sun was setting behind West Mountain, and the bridge was silhouetted against the sky from where I stood below it. I wanted to talk to her, tell her how I was doing. I wanted somehow to go back, to be standing there as her car plunged into the water, so I could stop it. Or save her. Or go with her. But the river just ran quietly under the bridge, and the sun sank lower and lower behind the mountain, and I got cold. So I jogged back home.

# CHAPTER 18

I STUCK TO MADISON'S plan of not running against the clock except in meets and won my first three races going away. I ran both distances—mile and two-mile—but I concentrated on the two. Eight laps didn't seem like all that much after all the miles I'd put in getting ready, and there wasn't a whole lot of competition because no one around the league was training the way I was. It felt good. I paid very little attention to time. That wasn't hard because I didn't know a good time from a hot rock. Madison was still convinced that I'd never run into those seemingly unbreakable barriers if I didn't know what they were.

I didn't get a chance to compete in Trout for the first month because there are never any home meets scheduled for the beginning of the season on account of the snow. Regular track workouts were still being held on the back roads. Two of our shot-putters were swallowed up by jelly rolls and never heard from again. At least that's what Carter said.

I wasn't all that anxious to perform at home anyway because the final count wasn't in on who thought I was just a mixed-up kid and who hated my guts, and I didn't think too much of the possibility of running my best two-mile only to be booed by the few people watching.

I rode to the meets with Floyd just as we'd planned, much to the envy of most of the team, but I was never really alienated at meets. At the first one, in Riordon, I found an empty spot on the infield; but Carter came over, plopped his spikes down on the ground beside me, and said, "Hell with Jasper. Word has it we're going to have to think for ourselves when we get out of here."

Pretty soon about half the team was there, and things were a lot like old times. Even Boomer came over. He didn't say much, but at least he'd given up the idea of cramming a banana down my throat and then reaching down there to peel it. Since the funeral he's given me a little room. I guess there was something in my agony that rang a bell in his own life. I wouldn't push it, but it feels like the extreme danger may be over.

The fourth meet of the season was scheduled to be run here, and a streak of luck and good warm weather teamed up to melt all the snow off the track. It wouldn't be fast, but at least we wouldn't have to wade around it. Madison borrowed a pickup and brought extra dirt in to fill in the potholes and raked and dragged it every night after workout until he had it looking pretty good. The meet was a league invitational, involving all eight teams. Actually all the meets are league invitationals—I mean, they call it an invitational, but everyone gets invited—so by this time I'd run against the same guys three times and beaten them three times. Trout had by far the best team. Lednecky scares all the football players into coming out, so we have a lot more depth. Besides, four of the schools that don't have as much snow as we do have baseball, so that cuts considerably into their track personnel. Anyway, we were scheduled to win all the meets. We couldn't take the sprints or the long jump, though, because Washington had those events covered like a blanket. He'd grab a big lead in the first ten yards, then pull away. Carter had never been shut out so many times in a row, and they ran all the same events. And that put Boomer third. Naturally it just served as proof of what he'd said all along: Niggers are fast and therefore stupid and yellow and will knife your old man in service station rest rooms.

The Friday morning of the meet I stopped to pick up Carter on the way to school. Through the year we shared that little bit of tradition, and sometimes I think I'd never have gotten through without it. He's one of the most constant things in my life. Doesn't always back my position, but he never tries to take it away from me either. It's one thing to have adults helping you out and giving you direction, but it's another to have someone like Carter who's going through a lot of the same things you are and holding it together with some style.

As you might imagine, Carter doesn't get too hyped up about track meets. About all track does for him, besides give him a pain in the butt, is keep him in condition, but he was really jacked up about my distance running. In the first three meets he was more excited than I was when I won, and that's pretty excited. After each race he'd come screaming and jumping up to me, pounding on my back and being completely obnoxious. I loved it. At Tamarack Falls he even ran over and dragged the reporter for the Tamarack *Times* back over to get some pictures of me standing with my hands on my knees, gasping for air. He really helped me get back into the groove, back to the way things had always been.

We parked the pickup in front of the school and went to English. Nobody gets as excited about track as they do football or basketball, so Friday mornings are like most others, but this one was different. Jasper's voice came over the intercom and took me by complete surprise. "All students will meet on the front lawn in ten minutes for a special dedication ceremony in honor of Becky Sanders."

I just froze. Carter scribbled a note. They were planting a tree in Becky's memory and setting a bronze plaque in concrete beside it. The reason I didn't know anything about it was that it was planned during the week I was hauling into Stibnite, and they were just waiting for Jasper to come up with the wording for the plaque and have it made.

The tree sounded like a good idea. The plaque sounded like a bad idea if Jasper was supposed to come up with the wording. And I could already hear his dedication speech banging around in my head, so I decided not to go. Besides, I didn't want to cry and make a big dummy out of myself.

When the bell rang, I headed for the gym, and met Madison in the hall. "Muscle spasm in my leg," I said. "Okay if I put some heat on it?"

Madison was no dummy. He said, "Sure, want some company?"

"Naw, it's okay."

I went on out to the gym and up into the training room, to find Carter sitting on the table. "Let's have a look at that leg," he said with a big grin.

I dropped my pants and lay down on my stomach, while he felt my gastroc. "Um-hmm," he said. "Muscle spasm. Better put a little heat on it."

"You turdburger, you heard me."

"Heard what? Quiet. This is a delicate procedure."

He rubbed a little analgesic on the leg, covered it with cotton, and wrapped it with an Ace bandage. "In case someone wants proof," he said.

I sat up on the table. "Thanks, Doc," I said. "You're right, I shouldn't be alone."

"No lie," he said. "Doctor's orders."

"I wish they wouldn't do that."

"Doctors?" he said. "Issue orders?"

"No, peckerwood. I wish they wouldn't keep trying to remember Becky the way I know they're going to. It always seems like they miss the point."

"What was the point, Louie?"

"I don't know, but it wasn't that she was going to be valedictorian or that she was a cheerleader or in Honor Society or any of that."

"It was for them," he said. "Buddy, I hate to tell you this, but it's not up to you to say what Becky Sanders stood for." He sounded like Norm or Dakota. Bastard's smart.

"Yeah," I said. "I guess you're right. But Jasper just uses that kind of stuff. He'll make it sound like she stood for all the things he stands for, and I *know* that's not right."

"Can't argue with you there," he said. "I wouldn't be surprised if the plaque says, 'Becky Sanders builds young men.'"

I laughed.

"But it's not important," he said, "and the best thing you can do is forget it."

Carter was right, of course. It wasn't important. But it sure bugged the hell out of me. When I went home for lunch, I purposely avoided the plaque because I didn't even want to know what it said. I forgot about it completely during the afternoon, while I was getting ready for my races, and afterward, when guys were slapping me on the back and shaking my hand and giving me five because I won the two-mile by more than two hundred yards. I was close to qualifying for regionals, according to Carter, who already had my entry forms filled out for the Olympics.

But I remembered it again as I sat in the training room, waiting for the rest of the guys to clear out of the locker so I could shower without contaminating them. Lednecky was in his office, working on some plays for next year, so I couldn't use the coaches' shower.

When everyone was gone, I went down and soaked myself for a long time. I turned on three of the nozzles and lay down with my butt covering the drain so the bottom would fill up. You get little square hickies on your butt from the drain suction when you do that, but it really feels good to let all that hot water pound down on you. 'Course then you have to stand up and wash off really good to keep those strange and exotic fungi that grow between people's toes from cropping up in your armpits or someplace.

I dressed and walked through the deserted school building and out across the lawn to the pickup. Usually Carter waits for me, but he had to go do something for his mom. I saw the tree, a dinky little thing with very few leaves. It will grow. The plaque caught the sun and flashed in the corner of my eye as I was about to get in, so I went over to see it.


BECKY SANDERS 1964–1982


THS 1-2-3-4 Cheerleader 2-3-4 Student Council 2-3-4
Class President 2 Honor Society 2-3-4 Band 1-2-3-4

Cougarettes 1-2-3-4 Girls' State 3 Carnival Queen 3
Class Play 4 Valedictorian 4

"A shining and joyous example of all that Trout High
School aspires to be"

Anthony Jasper
Superintendent/Principal
Trout High School    1982

Now I didn't mind having her yearbook stats there at all,
and if you could forget what Jasper aspires Trout High
School to be, the quote was even tolerable. But that ego-
maniac had the au-freaking-dacity to sign it. His name
was there *in his handwriting!* I'm sorry, but that was a
little much for me. I mean, Becky didn't even hate him.
She felt sorry for him.

I went home. Norm and Brenda congratulated me on
my victory, fed me, and we sat around shooting the bull
until Norm dozed off and Brenda went into the kitchen to
knit and listen to the radio. Then I picked Norm's keys off
the dining room table, hopped into the pickup, and drove
down to the station, where I got the sledgehammer we use
to repair tire trucks. It was about eleven. I drove to a spot
about a block away from the school, parked the pickup,
and walked the rest of the way, swinging the hammer
around to the side and over my head. It's possible I was
whistling "John Henry." When I got to the schoolyard, I
went over to the plaque and swung four or five times as

| 175

hard as I could, blasting it loose from the concrete. Then I picked it up, jogged back to the pickup, and drove out to the bridge, where I chucked it into the river. As I whipped a tight U-turn and headed home, I could almost hear Becky laughing.

# CHAPTER 19

B ECKY MAY HAVE BEEN laughing, but Anthony Jasper, Superintendent/Principal, Trout High School 1982, sure as hell wasn't. He was hacked. I've never seen him so hacked. Monday morning he didn't leave the customary notice on the bulletin board stating his desire for an audience with me. He met me at the front entrance.

He said, "Into my office!" as I walked by.

"Yes, sir." I hustled up the stairs, through the outer office, and into the inner sanctum.

The door slammed, and Jasper stalked around behind his desk. "Sit down!" he said.

I sat. He didn't.

"By God, Banks," he said, and the look in his eye was almost murderous, "I don't know what you think you're trying to do, but before this day is over, if I have my way, you'll be out of this school for good!"

I dug down deep for my best surprised look and said, "Why? What's going on?"

"You know damn good and well what's going on," he said. "Look me in the eye and tell me you honestly don't know what I'm talking about."

I looked him in the eye and said, "I honestly don't know what you're talking about."

"You're a liar!" he said. "On top of everything else, you're a liar. I feel sorry for your parents, Louie. I really do. Parents have an obligation to protect their kids, but you must push that to the very edge."

I put my hands up. "Look," I said, "I'd be more than happy to have you call Norm and Brenda and get them up here—"

He waved me off. "Where were you last night?"

"Home."

"All night?"

"Yes, sir. Oh, no. I went out for a drive about ten-thirty or eleven." Just in case he checked with the folks. They didn't know anything about it.

"Where to?"

"Around the lake a ways. Why? What happened? Whatever it was, I didn't do it."

"Somebody vandalized the plaque we dedicated to Becky Sanders. I know it was you. I mean, who else would do a thing like that?"

My voice rose. "Are you crazy?" I settled back. "Excuse me, but why would I do something like that? I thought it was a neat idea. Really."

His eyes narrowed. "If you thought it was a 'neat' idea, as you put it, why didn't you attend the ceremony? You think I'm stupid? I notice things like that."

I didn't address whether or not I thought he was stupid. I just looked at the floor in front of my feet and said, "I didn't go to the ceremony because it still hurts too much and I didn't want to make a fool out of myself."

He just stared.

"What did they do to it?" I asked. "Mark it up or something? Can't it be fixed?"

"No. They broke it out of the concrete."

"Geez," I said. "With what?"

"I don't know what you did it with. Probably a sledge-hammer. Don't play games with me, Banks; you're in a lot of trouble. I'll get the law in on this if I have to."

"I didn't do it," I said, my voice rising slightly again. "Really. I've done a lot of stupid things this year, but that wasn't one of them."

"That's right," he said. "You've done a *lot* of stupid things. There's no one else who would have any motive."

Motive. I was determined to stay cool. There wasn't a shred of evidence. I even washed off the hammer when I took it back. "What motive? I mean, why would I do a stupid thing like that?"

"Why would you make a shambles out of her funeral? Why would you make that ridiculous scene on the football field and then lie to back it up? You're a sick boy, Louie. If I were Norm, I'd have you tested."

"I was out of my head at the funeral," I said. "I'd never do anything like that in my right mind."

Jasper's eyes narrowed again. His voice went low, and he pointed his famous index finger right at my heart. "Banks, I know I'm right, and I'm going to prove it."

"I'm sorry, sir," I said, "but there isn't any proof because *I didn't do it*."

"Until I do, you're suspended."

"I'll take *that* to the school board," I said. "I haven't learned an awful lot from government class this year—believe me I haven't—but I have learned that I'm innocent until proved guilty. Even you are bound by that. You can't just accuse me of something and make it stand." I sat forward. "Really, Mr. Jasper. I'd swear on a stack of Bibles that I didn't do it."

He just erupted. "A stack of Bibles doesn't mean a damn thing to you!" he screamed. I had him on the run. "I heard you at the funeral! God knows what is sacred to you!"

"Then I'll swear on the Koran! Or the Bhagavad-Gita! Or a yearbook! I didn't do it!"

"Go to your class," he said. "Get out of my sight."

I stood up to leave. "Excuse me, sir," I said, "but did you say it was knocked completely out of its concrete base?"

He glared.

I shook my head. "Whoever did it must be an animal. That thing looked like it was really in there. Maybe you should ask Boomer—"

"Get out of here!"

I hustled off to class. My suspension was obviously a bluff.

I wasn't that comfortable around school that day. A lot of people must have shared Jasper's opinion that I'd busted up the plaque because not many spoke to me and I could feel them looking. Carter stopped me after English and said if I did, he didn't want to know about it, so I told him the same thing I'd told Jasper. I said I knew it looked like I did it, but I didn't, that I'd like to find the guy, too.

Madison never said a word about it. He was bound and determined to coach me in track and leave the rest of my life to me. I was in the training room dressing down after school when he came in to change.

"Heard a rumor," he said.

"You, too?"

He shook his head. "This rumor's about track. I heard Washington has been training for a week to run the two-mile."

"Oh, God!" I said. "Where'd you hear that?"

"John Lamaar, his coach. Says he needs the challenge."

"When?"

"Lamaar says he thinks he'll run it at district, as his fourth event. He's going to stay out of the relay."

I thought for a second. "He can't be in that good shape," I said. "Not with only three weeks' training at the outside."

"Maybe not," Madison said, "but he's a tremendous athlete, and he's obviously not afraid of a challenge." He laced his shoes. "You know, we haven't had a distance man qualify for regionals since 1968, when Dave Orwell qualified in the mile. That's fourteen years." He winked. "Just a thought," he said, and walked out.

I trained the rest of the week like a man possessed, as Mrs. Kjack is fond of saying about the way Mark Robeson plays the accordion. The first-place finisher at district goes to regionals, no matter what the time, and I didn't even know what the qualifying time was. I wanted to go as the number one man from our district.

The weather was with me, the ground was dry almost everywhere, and the days were getting longer, so I had more time to work out. Running hills got to be my forte. I figured if I could really stride out and keep the pressure on going up a long, steep hill, a flat, oval track would be a cinch. I'd start on the short course up by the lake, take off into the hills at the old cemetery, and run ridge after ridge until I thought I couldn't take it. Then I'd run back. The thing that ran through my mind most was the mile at the beginning of football season. At the end, when I'd given it everything I had, Boomer just spurted past me. I could just see Washington striding out the last fifteen yards after following me for seven and seven-eighths laps, to pass me like I was a traffic cop.

Friday. The district meet was being held at Salmon River because they have a rubberized asphalt track, fastest in the league. That gave Washington the advantage of a home crowd, which was bad because he's a showman all the way.

I got to the meet ahead of the team because the bus had a flat tire. We passed them about thirty miles out of Salmon River, waving and blasting our horn. I was in a hurry to get there, so I'd have plenty of time to warm up.

Several of the other teams were there when we pulled in, and I went over and found an empty spot in the infield and plopped down my gear. I already wore my sweats and uniform because I couldn't shower with the team after the meet, so there was no use in bringing clothes. I sat down to put short spikes in my shoes—you can't use long ones on asphalt—and as I was finishing the second one, I noticed a shadow. Looking up behind me, I saw Washington, standing with his hands on his hips, grinning.

"Comin' after you today, my man," he said.

I smiled. "That's what I hear. Gonna have to come hard," I said. "Hey, how come you're tryin' to steal my show?"

"Just wanna see what you got," he said, "besides guts. I been watchin' you run; you're my hero. Got to take you on."

I nodded, squinting into the sun. That wasn't logic I was familiar with. "I'm glad, I guess. Maybe we should meet on a neutral track, though, for your sake. You hear that hometown crowd you might get too excited. Too much adrenaline." I pounded my chest. "Gotta watch out for your heart."

Washington looked around at the maybe fifty diehard track fans—mostly parents and a relatively small part of the Salmon River student body—and laughed. "Doubt I'll be hearin' much more than the blood poundin' in my ears," he said. "Two miles's a long ways."

I got up and we started jogging.

"So what's it really like around here for you?"

"You mean, 'cause I'm black?"

"Yeah, I guess that's what I mean."

"Well," he said, "I didn't have a date for the prom, if you know what I mean, but folks treat me pretty good, I'd say."

I nodded. "You in shape for this?" I asked. "Eight laps's a long ways, like you said." So much for my feeble attempt to psyche him out.

"I'll get by," he said. "Listen, Louis, my man. Got to tell you somethin'. Lots of guys who run against me give up. Think I'm too fast and just give up. I don't want you doin' that."

I started to say I wouldn't.

"This ain't my distance," he said, and broke into a grin. "This *ain't* my distance. But I'm gonna give it what I got. What I'm tellin' you is you give it what you got, you might take me."

I said I'd give it what I got.

"Listen"—he stopped me—"I came over to tell you two things. Don't let me psyche you, and"—he paused—"however it turns out, you got my respect, and not a lot of dudes can say that. I know what happened when young Mr. Boomer tried to make a dead nigger out of me. Okay?"

I said okay.

He smiled. "Don't want to burn myself out with this warmin' up," he said. "Catch you later." He slapped my hand and headed to the infield.

I'd never competed against anyone before who didn't just want to beat my butt and go home. It's funny; besides really wanting to win, I felt like I owed him a good race.

I jogged another easy mile and a half and went over to let Floyd massage my legs, wondering how this all was

184

going to turn out. Floyd was sort of getting to be my personal trainer. All the time we rode to meets he never said a word about any of the crap I pulled all year long. We just talked track and a little about my future. He was pretty sure there were some small colleges around that would give me a partial scholarship to run cross-country and track. He wished he'd done that. It's a little late, but I'm looking into it.

Washington won the hundred and the two-twenty going away, and Carter just slapped him on the butt after each race and shook his head. Boomer sneered. When the first call was given for the two-mile, I trotted over to Madison and said, "Earn your pay. Coach me."

"Run *your* race," he said. "Run loose like always. You'll have to run a fast first mile to wear him down. Your best bet is to be far enough ahead on the last lap that he can't even make a run at you. He's fast. Ask Sampson." He rubbed my legs. "I don't think he can go out ahead of you. He hasn't run it enough to know what he can handle. If he does, you still run your race; he may be trying to psyche you. Just don't panic, no matter what. You have the advantage of knowing your limit."

The gun sounded. Washington was smart. He wasn't about to kill himself off by taking the lead. He figured if he could stay within a reasonable distance for seven laps, he could outdo me with sheer speed on the last one. I knew he'd do exactly that unless I broke him, so I set a good pace. Madison hollered out my times at the end of each quarter, and they were well under my usual; the first mile was my best ever, and I still had a lot left. Never once was Washington far enough back that I couldn't hear his spikes pounding the track.

I opened up a little on the fifth lap, hoping to catch him in a midway slump and break him, but he hung in. The thought that he could stay with me no matter what pace I set crept into my mind, but I banished it and picked up.

So did he.

Since I couldn't shake him, I decided I had to burn him out on laps six and seven so he wouldn't have a final sprint. I mean, he *had* to have a limit. The old familiar burning deep in my bowels, a constant companion during most of my hard workouts, made its presence felt, and I welcomed it, knowing he had to be feeling it, too. I coped with it, as usual, by telling myself it didn't hurt half as much as when Leo Frazier accidentally fouled me off with that baseball bat. I picked up more, concentrating on relaxing my upper body—especially my arms.

Starting into the eighth lap, I had about half a stride on him and poured it on. The first two-twenty we went stride for stride. Going into the final turn, I had the inside, so he stayed close right at my shoulder. I could almost see him out of the corner of my eye but refused to look, to break my concentration. I knew he was hurting. He'd have taken me by now if he wasn't.

My legs ached. My lungs wanted to explode. He reached for his kick, but it wasn't quite there. I strode out and counted to myself, increasing the speed of the cadence to fight him off. I couldn't shake him, but he couldn't kick it in. I saw the tape, and out of the corner of my eye I saw his hand. Blackness closed in from the sides as I lunged for the tape and felt its casual pressure across my chest. I stumbled to the track, vaguely aware of the asphalt scraping my hands, knees, and shoulders as I tumbled over and over.

I heard myself screaming and moaning as my legs cramped into a million bizarre knots, and then, "Relax, man. Relax," as Carter slowly straightened them and worked at the knots while talking me down. Madison was there, too, and Floyd was coming with his car and a stretcher. I looked over and saw Washington lying back flat on the grass just off the track. His coach was telling him to jog it off, but he just smiled and waved him away.

"I'm okay," I said. "I just need to walk around a little."

Blood oozed from the abrasions on my knees and left shoulder. My hands felt like I'd grabbed a fistful of bumblebees. I tried to stand, but my legs knotted immediately with the first movement.

"Relax, man," Washington said, looking over at me from his spot on the infield. "They comin' to get you."

I started to laugh. "What the hell are you doing alive?" I said.

"I didn't have it, man. If I could've pushed myself like you, I'da beat your butt by six blocks." He got up, came over, and put his palm out flat, and I slapped it. Instant pain filled mine.

"Incredible," Carter said from behind me as he helped lift me onto the stretcher.

When I was secure on it, Madison said, "We just want to take you over to the hospital and let a doctor have a

187

look. Floyd'll drive you over, and I'll get someone to ride in back with you."

"Let me go, man," Washington said. "I got no relay today." He shook his head. "Ain't got nothin' after that."

Both my time and place qualified me for regionals, and I trained like a madman for the next two weeks after the doctor found nothing wrong that a weekend's rest wouldn't heal. The first week I increased my distances by half and pressured myself to the brink of exhaustion. The second week I tapered off until, on Friday, I felt like I could beat the world. Unfortunately there were three other guys who could also beat the world—and me. I finished fourth; the world, fifth. Only the top three places go on to state, so that wrapped up my high school track career. Washington went on to finish first in state in the hundred and long jump and second in the two-twenty. He hadn't even bothered to compete in the two-mile at regionals, though his time qualified him. That guy's a star.

The week after regionals Jasper called me into his office again. He was actually pretty friendly at first, said maybe he had jumped to conclusions about me being the mad hammer man, and told me he was planning to replace the plaque, and maybe I could help him. He said even though I didn't do it, was there some reason that I could think of that someone else might have?

I said maybe they were offended by what it said or maybe that he signed it. Maybe it should be from everybody. Or maybe the plaque should say "In Memoriam" with Becky's name on it. You know, let the tree do the talking.

He nodded and said he understood. I think probably he did.

We had commencement tonight, so I guess it's almost over. I hope so, it's about time. Something happened up there that will probably stand out in my memory almost as much as Becky's death. It's hard to believe the highs and lows you go through. After the prayers were all said and Senator Hansen gave his speech and Carter gave the salutatory address and we had a minute's silence for Becky, Jasper and the senator and Norm, as chairman of the school board, lined up to give out the diplomas. I was third, because I'm third in the alphabet, thanks to Jen and Dick Aardvarrsen, and when Jasper called my name, I stood up, walked over and shook his hand and Senator Hansen's hand, and then moved in front of Norm. He handed me my diploma, and I moved my tassel from one side to the other. Then he put out his hand and said in a real quiet voice, "Son, I wish there were some way I could tell you how proud I am."

I started to shake his hand, and then I just lost it. I threw my arms around his neck and burst into tears. I don't know whether he was embarrassed or not, but I just couldn't help it. Behind us the gym was dead quiet. I took a deep breath and turned around to see Carter, standing, giving me thumbs-up.

I learned a lot this year, in spite of the fact that I was going to school. I learned some about friendship and a whole lot about love and that there's no use being honorable with dishonorable men. There's nothing they can do to you when you don't care anymore. I learned to accept myself even though I'm not Clint Eastwood or Joe Montana or Carter Sampson, and that you can get through almost anything if you have people around you who care about you. And I learned that when all is said and done, you're responsible for every damn thing you do. Most important, I learned how jacked up you can get just being alive, and what a vicious, miserable, ugly thing death is. I'm going to stay away from it if I can.

A few things I didn't learn. I didn't learn to like people who don't like me, and I didn't learn not to push my luck. About a week and a half ago they set a new plaque in concrete beside Becky's tree. Jasper didn't take my advice; it was a duplicate of the other one. What Jasper did do was camp out overnight in his office for about a week with a .22 loaded with birdshot, waiting for me to show. But I've learned patience. He's tucked away at home in his own bed tonight, visions of beating me to death with a blunt instrument dancing in his head. In about five minutes I'm going down to the station to get the hammer.